JUST ONE *Moment*

JAMI ROGERS

For Dana and Mary
I wouldn't be where I am today without your support and encouragement.

JUST ONE *Moment*

JAMI ROGERS

JUST ONE MOMENT

THE BLACK ALCOVE SERIES BOOK 4

JAMI ROGERS

CHAPTER ONE

Luke

The urge to shout "fuck it" is at the tip of my tongue at least once a day.

I never actually say it, though. All it would cause is a whole lot more pain in my mother's heart. I'd rather claw my eyes from their sockets than ever witness my mother shed another tear.

I'd do anything for my family. Even if it means stopping by my mom's house in between jobs to make sure she and my sisters are doing alright. I really should be using this hour to relax, because working two jobs—one that I am part owner in —and being a full-time art major student is exhausting. Or I should study for an exam I have coming up next week to end the summer semester. I'll be the first to admit it that "free time" isn't part of my vocabulary these days, but I struggle to choose which is more important: living the life I want or making sure my family has the life they deserve.

I park my 1968 Dodge Charger RT on the curb outside my

mother's house and head inside. A chirp sounds behind me as I press the lock button and stuff the keys into my pocket. The car's bright, cherry-apple red stands out in the old, dingy neighborhood.

Mom's new neighbors stay up late playing loud music, random cars are always coming and going, and they use their front yard as a trash can. Not to mention the excessive amount of arguing that happens in the middle of the night. I hate to judge, but the idea of my family living near these people worries me, and I'm pretty convinced that it's drug deal behavior at the house on their left. Locking my car is a must. Especially when building this car back to life was the last thing my father and I did together. It's my final memory of being with him, and I'll never let it go.

"Lucas."

My mother, Julianne Warren, greets me in her soft, warm tone as I step through the door. I give her a full, tight hug—the way I always do when I see her—and she smiles up at me. It's her normal smile, but there's still a darker shade under her eyes. *I hope she starts sleeping better soon.*

"How many times do I have to tell you that you do not have to check up on me?"

She can tell me as much as she wants, but I'll never listen. Ever since my dad passed away, things have been hard on all of us. Between working extra shifts at the hospital, making sure twin thirteen-year-old girls have rides to get where they need to be, food to eat, and still being a mom who's actively in their lives for sports and whatever else they do, Mom has it the worst of all. She pretends it doesn't take a toll on her and my sisters, but I can see it in the way her eyes wrinkle at the crease more each time I visit.

"I have no idea what you're talking about," I tell her, grinning because it's how I reply every time. She swats at my arm and rolls her eyes. "You act just like your father." Laughing, she heads for the dining room. "Your sisters are in the living room. Don't get them all wound up before you leave."

This time it's my turn to laugh. "I never do that. Those two feed off each other."

"Yeah, okay," she says, her dark hair swooshing to the side as she disappears through the entry into the kitchen.

I toe off my shoes and hang my coat on a free peg by the door. It's a wooden coat rack that my dad made when I was seven. There are two pegs lying on the floor. How three women can break those off I have no idea, but I make a mental note to fix it later.

I step quietly into the living room and spy Brandy sprawled out on the couch with her phone in her hands and Shea sitting on the floor with her back against the couch as she reads from the book clenched between her fingers. They both have rich brown hair that falls to the middle of their backs, bright green eyes, and freckles that sprinkle just over their noses. If it weren't for the fact that Shea prefers her glasses to contacts, people would never be able to tell them apart. It amazes me how much they look like our mother. I have the same dark hair, only buzzed short, and I have blue eyes, like my dad.

I can't believe how much they're growing up. These next few years are going to be some wild ones for Mom.

"I'm actually impressed the TV isn't on right now," I say.

"Luke!" Brandy cheers and jumps off the couch to hug me. "I was hoping you'd stop by. I have a question for you."

"Don't you even dare ask him!" Shea looks up from her

book, glaring at Brandy. It's definitely a look that would make me think twice.

"Well, he is a guy, Shea. He'll probably have some great advice."

Oh no.

"Shea likes a boy, but she doesn't know how to get his attention. I told her to just go up to him and say hey, and if he walks away then move on to the next one."

Move on to the next one?

"Tell me once when that advice has worked for you," Shea snaps.

I sit on the back of the couch as both girls are now standing in front of me with their hands on their hips as they face each other. Mom must be loving these new teen years.

"Considering guys have never walked away from me, I'm certain it will work," Brandy says.

What the?

"Whoa," I say, shaking my head and holding my hands up. "I do have advice." They both direct their bodies toward me and cross their arms. I look them both in the eyes before I continue. "Neither of you should be thinking of anything that involves boys."

"Oh, come on, Luke, we're thirteen now. It's totally normal," Shea says.

"Yea, I mean I've already been kissed. This is just the first—"

"Mom!" I yell, cutting Brandy off. No way I'm going to let her finish that sentence. Who cares that I'm twenty-four years old and hollering for my mother like a kid?

"Why are you yelling?" Mom asks, holding a pan and towel in her hands as she dries.

"Um, because Brandy and Shea are going to be home-schooled from now on," I answer.

"Seriously!"

"Men!"

I'm not sure who said what as they walk away from me to resume their previous spots, but I don't like the tone from either of them. Mom just laughs.

"Come help me with these dishes. I know you're headed somewhere, so you better get in here quick."

Anything is better than listening to my baby sisters' talk about boys and kissing. As much as I hated being an only child and loved it when my parents announced the "oops twins," I do not enjoy moments like that one.

I'm about to cross through the doorway to the kitchen when the last family photo we took with Dad catches my eye. His hand was over my shoulder, and I rub that same spot automatically. That was my first day of freshman year. Everyone had to wait more than an hour for me that day. Mom was upset because when I *did* arrive I had paint all over my arms and face, and my family had to wait for me to scrub it off. Dad said if holding me down himself was how they'd get the picture, that was what he would do. That was also the moment Dad reminded me how strong he was.

"Can you believe it's already been more than a year?" Mom whispers to me. Her eyes find mine, and I don't miss the flicker of her gaze from me to my sisters before she nudges me into the kitchen.

"Their school is hosting a father-daughter dance at the start of this next year. Shea isn't handling it very well, and Brandy is pretending it doesn't bother her."

Of course this would happen just when things were

starting to be normal again and not everything they saw reminded them of Dad. I have to look away from Mom; I can see the glaze in her eyes already.

"What if …"

My words trail off. Mom is slowly sliding something under the computer sitting on the table. Bold red capital letters that say "final notice" on not only one but two pieces of mail are peeking out from under her fingers. "What's this? What happened to the money I gave you last week?" I ask, my hands gripping the back of a chair as I lean forward, waiting for her answer. She hesitates and then takes a seat.

"The girls want to be more involved with school and academics this year, but prices have gone up."

My teeth grind together as I take a breath. "Then I'll bring you more money."

"No, Luke, you've done so much this last year. I can't let you sacrifice any more of your life on us."

If Dad's life insurance had covered more than their debt, the Warren woman would be just fine. But it didn't, and I won't let them struggle.

"I'm a grown man, Mom, and I am going to take care of my mother and sisters." I step forward to kiss the top of her head. "I have to get to work, but I'll be back tomorrow."

She doesn't say anything as I walk away, which is good. I don't want to argue with her today. It also saves me from not having to discuss the reason I came here in the first place. The one thing I have been dreading for the last few weeks.

It's time we sell the bookstore. My father's store.

Skylar

Being homeless is exhausting.

I push against the glass door of the motel's entrance where I've been staying the last week. Chu is working behind the receptionist desk, like he always is. He doesn't stand very tall, and his eyes can barely see over the top of the wooden counter as he watches me step inside. His black hair is combed over today, and he has on another oversized, bright yellow, short-sleeve button-up shirt. He always looks as though he's headed for a luau. He definitely isn't going to find any of those in Wyoming. Maybe it's that damn coconut candle playing tricks on his mind. I swear he buys them in bulk.

"Good evening, Mr. Chu," I greet him with the same polite tone as always. "Another gorgeous summer night, isn't it?"

"Miss Sky, you no pay this week's rent again." His familiar beady eyes ignore my question and flash to the opposite corner of the room. My red backpack sits propped up with clothes sticking out the top as though someone didn't take the time to care. Which, clearly, they didn't. "You no pay, you no sleep here."

"Just a couple more days, I promise. I'm working on finding a new job." It's the truth. After another night at the diner where no one wanted to sit in my section and five tables requested a different waitress, I finally came to the conclusion I need a new job.

I've avoided going to The Black Alcove bar, where a friend told me I should apply if I want more money. I have no bartending skills. In fact, I don't have many skills for a lot of things. Money does that to a person. Being catered to my entire life has done me no favors for my current situation, but the fact I could be going without another dinner tonight is almost enough to make me suck it up and apply.

"No," he says, a fast answer and solid reminder that no one is catering to me anymore.

"You can't seriously kick me out again." I march toward my bag, swinging it over my shoulder and looping each arm through a strap. Just like my polite tone, this conversation is becoming routine for us. Every other week I can make rent; the other weeks I can't and am out on my ass.

"Find another place to sleep, Miss Sky." You'd think by now he would have compassion for a twenty-two-year-old woman with no place to go. "You bring me money and I let you come back."

"Yeah, yeah, I know."

Another sleepless night in the park won't kill me.

I step back out into the evening sun and head for the gym. Thank god I can manage to keep up on my monthly membership there. The locker I use is the perfect size for my backpack, and they have showers stocked with shampoo, conditioner, and body wash for their members. I can use as many towels I want, and they have hair dryers by every sink. It's not a lot, but it saves me money in that area. I only have to buy makeup or clothes if I need new ones. I've mastered the "I'm your guest and forgot my toothbrush and toothpaste" enough times at the fancier hotels that I'm stocked up for a few months. The only thing I need now is for the gym to offer me a place to sleep and to never raise their rate over forty bucks a month.

Forty bucks I might not be able to afford either if I don't find a new job.

If I get this job at the BA, as everyone has nicknamed it, it better earn me the money I need to get my own place soon. There's no way I can survive overnighters in the park when winter comes around, and being as it's the last week of August, I'm pretty sure winter is going to sneak up on me. I sure don't want to be sleeping at motel Chu forever either, but until I decide what I'm doing with my life, this *is* my life. The only thing I know for sure is that I will never go back to what I should be calling home. It was more like a prison.

"Hey, girl, you need a ride?"

Beth Moyer, the first local to claim me as her friend, slows to a stop in her Nitro. Her red hair waves out the window with the light breeze. Being friends with someone who grew up here and knows everyone has drawn some unwanted attention to me. Sooner or later, people are going to pick up on the fact that I don't have a home. I'd like to resolve that part of my life before they have the time to find out. It still shocks me that I've made it three months, but I also have a feeling it's all about to blow up and everyone is going to know. They would all rush to help me, and that isn't a bad thing, but I don't think I could handle it. I don't want to be pitied.

"No thanks, I'm just headed to the gym," I answer.

Becoming friends with Beth and Alex, whose boyfriend told me to stop into the BA for a job after I admitted to working at the town diner, has made me feel more at home here where I have no home than back in Seattle where I have a family who thinks zeros in a bank account make you better than everyone else. Still, I can't take advantage of my new friends and let them drive me around. That's the whole point of being here. To learn to take care of myself and find out who I am in the process—that's the short version. I made a list and everything.

"Ugh, no wonder you're so skinny. You walk everywhere."

Skinny? Shoot. I have no bed and no food tonight. *Thanks for reminding me, Beth.*

"Yeah, don't tell anyone my secret," I say, winking and continuing on my way.

"Okay, fine, I won't give you a ride, but when are you going to come into the BA for a job? Conner told you to come in like *for-ev-er* ago."

"I was thinking tomorrow."

I keep walking and her car continues to creep along next to me. It would probably make the most sense to just take her up on her offer, but come on—since when in the last few months or even year did I choose the easy route? Nope, I have to make life as complicated as can be.

"Finally!" she cheers out the window, removing her hands from the wheel to clap.

A horn honks, and I trip myself as I jump from the noise.

"Jackass!" Beth hollers behind her. "I'll see you there!" she shouts to me and then flashes a grin before driving off. Her middle finger also went up between her seats for the guy behind her.

Beth doesn't waste time getting to the point in any topic. She knows everyone in this town, and she is always willing to help out any way she can. As many times as I've seen her volunteer to help someone, she can't make any time for herself. If I could give her advice on anything in life without a ton of follow-up questions, it would be that she needs to take care of herself first. If she doesn't, she'll end up like me, and this isn't the life I'd wish upon anyone.

I reach the gym, other members entering and exiting

through the sliding doors. Some have eager faces ready for a workout, and some look ready for a nap. The only actual workout I've done here is yoga, where I met both Alex and Beth. That's a class that will put you to sleep when it's over, for sure.

"Skylar!"

I twist to see who has called my name. Alex. Her blond hair shines against the sun, and she has a smile on, like always. Jake, her boyfriend's son, is next to her with a basketball tucked under his arm.

"What are you two up to today?" I ask, mainly directing the question toward Jake.

"Alex is gonna shoot some ball with me," he answers, switching the ball to rest under his other arm.

"That sounds fun."

"Do you want to join us?" Alex offers. I walk next to her and Jake as we head inside.

"Oh, no thank you, I have some things I have to do before it gets dark."

"All right, well, I bet we'll be here for a couple hours if you change your mind," she says over her shoulder, as she has to speed up her steps to follow Jake down the hall toward the basketball court.

Once I step into the locker room and adjust to the overwhelming smell of eucalyptus, I stash my bag in my locker and change into the only pair of sweat pants I packed in my dash to get out of my parents' home before they could see me and change my mind. Then again, I most likely could have walked right by them and they wouldn't have noticed.

I grab my hoodie and the list of goals I made when I left,

lock up, and leave the gym. I'll add *stop being homeless* to the list as soon as I find a pen.

I head to the coffee shop across from the town park where I read every section of the newspaper until they close at eleven, like I always do on the nights I have to sleep outside. After they close, I find the same tree next to the same bench and I sit back against the bark. *How did I let myself get here?*

I never let myself think for too long on whether I would prefer to be married into a family for money—which is exactly where my life was headed before I left—or out here alone, creating my own way. I could be in Washington right now, sitting on Mack's brown leather couch, snuggled under his arms as we watch a Nicholas Sparks movie … no wait … that's right … I'd be in the kitchen making dinner and cleaning his house like the good little wife he was trying turn me into while he sat in his office making a list of ways for me to more impressively present our relationship to the public. That memory alone makes it easier to decide that, homeless or not, this is where I'd rather be. Being me and only me, instead of the girl everyone thinks I should be.

CHAPTER TWO

Luke

"Ladies, ladies, ladies, how many times do I have to tell you that you can flutter your eyes, perk up your chest, and flash those award-winning smiles at me, but last call is last call?"

I wipe the counter in front of three women who are now pouting. One has long, black hair and skin so pale I'm not sure I didn't serve her too many drinks. The other, in the middle, has bright red hair like my good friend Beth, but it's not nearly as long and it doesn't look as well cared for, either. The last woman has short blonde hair and a silver dress so tight I'm afraid if she leans forward any more than she is now, her breasts might fall out.

Don't get me wrong, I love a nice rack, but I only want to see them on the woman I'm with and definitely only when it's intended for me. In this case, it might be the latter, but I'm not interested in her or any other girl. A man's got to have his priorities straight, and a woman in my life right now, one-night stand or not, isn't in the cards for me. I have a mother and two sisters who need my undivided attention.

The blonde leans forward and, yep, that's definitely a nip. I glance away. I'm a bartender and bookstore owner. They don't exactly go hand in hand, but they keep me busy. Like tonight—when I get off work here around midnight, I need to head to the bookstore and place the order I was working on before that trip to my mom's. The store isn't sold yet, so I have to maintain it until then. That means everything needs to go as smoothly as I can make it. People want to buy a store ready to open, not a fixer upper.

"Luke, you're always treating us so good when we come in here. Why not let us drink a little more and we can return the favor when you get off?"

Of course the blonde would be the one to make this suggestion. I'm pretty sure her name is Sally or Sandy. I should have this memorized by now because during the summer semester, these three have come in every Tuesday and Thursday night. They've already mentioned they will be here for the fall semester, too.

I settle the rag in my hands over my shoulder and lean forward on the bar.

"That's a tempting offer, but I already have plans after work." I shoot her a wink—I have to keep the customers coming back, after all—before I move on to my next piece of side work.

"Alright! Everyone out!" Beth shouts from the front door. She smiles at customers as they exit; the trio of ladies are the last to leave. Beth locks the door, turning to me when she's done. It's a look I've seen many times before. Because I grew up with her and now work with her, she knows me better than any other girl around. Maybe about as equal as Sara or Kelsey, a couple of our other closer friends, but still it's a look only the girls give me.

It says, "I'm about to give you a speech a mother would give."

"Stop." I chuckle and hold up my hand. "I know exactly what you're going to say, and I'm fine."

At a leisurely pace, she crosses her arms and heads toward the bar. From the corner of my eye, I see my buddy Conner approaching us with a crate of clean glasses.

"And what am I going to say?" Beth asks.

"That it's time I go out and have some fun. That I don't need to put all this pressure on myself. Same speech I get from you every night we've closed together for the last month." She's close enough now that I flick my wet hands at her, sprinkling her with water. She shrinks back and laughs.

"I hate it when you do that! And no, I was not going to say that."

"You weren't?"

"I was going to say that when you do decide to be my old friend Luke once again, please promise you will find a woman who is much more mature and a hundred percent less desperate than those three." She points to the door.

"I agree with Beth," Conner says from behind us, where he is stocking the shelf with dishware.

"I still think you should ask Skylar out," Beth adds. Her new friend has been in town for a while, but I have seen her less than a handful of times. She hardly ever talks and always seems on edge. She's hot, though. So that's a plus. But, like always, my friends forget where I'm at in my life.

"Maybe if I'm still single in a year or two, sure. I'll go for it."

"A year or two? At this rate, I can put money on yes, you will still be single. Come on, Luke," Beth pleads, but I just keep shaking my head and laughing. She doesn't give up easily.

"Dude, if you don't go on at least one date with her, Beth will never stop asking," Conner says. "At least do it for me so I can stop listening to her talk about it. Or better yet, why don't the two of you go out?"

"Ick, no," Beth answers. "Freshman year when we all went to our first high school party, Luke got so drunk trying to impress that senior chick, Annie or some crap, that he threw up all over me when I carried him to my car—which I had snuck out from my parents, might I remind you?—and then he threw up again in their car, *twice*." She wiggles two fingers at both me and Conner. "That was the day I put Luke in the forever friend zone."

Conner throws his head back with a laugh and I just grin. I did manage to get Annie's attention at the party that night, but that's only because I tripped over a table and fell on her right before Beth hauled me out.

"I wasn't that bad," I say.

I don't defend myself too much because it probably was that bad. That was my first party, and it definitely wasn't my last. High school was fun for me.

"Oh, please, I don't even want to get started on all the other times I drove you home. But lucky for you, the whole good guy thing you have going on continues to win me over."

"At least there's that," Conner adds. He glances my way, and the look in his eyes is one I saw numerous times growing up. It's a look that says, "You are not going to like what I'm about to say."

"You really should start going out again—maybe not drink or anything since you don't do that anymore, but it's been a while since we've all hung out," he says.

"Yeah, you've taken on so much in the last year, Luke. Have some fun again," Beth adds.

There is no such thing as fun when you're broke and have family who could benefit from your money more than you would.

"I appreciate the concern and knowing you are all here for me, but my family needs me, and without my dad, I can't let them down."

"No one thinks you have to—"

"I know. I want to, though."

Beth sighs with a half-smile before she heads to the back, and Conner pats me on the shoulder. "Head to the store and finish up. We can close here."

"Are you sure?" I ask.

They both nod.

"I'll be back in thirty minutes, tops," I say, backing toward the door and heading off in a jog for the two blocks to the bookstore.

This will give me a little extra time to check out the apartment over the store. I love my mom, but a man needs his space, so moving back home from my apartment across town isn't an option. I've been debating whether to just suck it up and keep bills and money tight or to move into the bookstore apartment, even though I know the room, after you take in account the kitchen space and bathroom, is only big enough to fit a twin-size bed and a small table. The walls need repainting, and the place has done nothing but collect dust over the last few years.

I need the money.

I can suck life up later. Right now, I need to do what's best for more than just me.

Skylar

This list of things I've never gotten to do just keeps getting longer: paint my nails pink, wear animal print, wear jean shorts with holes in them, oh, maybe I should add "color my hair." I mean, I love my blond hair, but changing it would be different, and who knows? Maybe I am the kind of person who dyes her hair all the time. Actually, I bet just a streak of some color, like bright blue or green, would be fun.

Who am I kidding? Would I being doing it because I can or because it's what I want? Okay, cross that one off. What's next?

Swear out loud.

Pretty sure I've done this since I've been here, but just in case …

"Shit!"

I pinch my lips together and lean back against the tree as I try to hide my smile. Not that anyone is watching me. It's probably midnight or later, and I doubt anyone heard me either. If I had a phone, I'd check the time, but when I left that night, I didn't want to chance anyone tracing my phone calls, so I left my phone behind. Kind of wish I hadn't done that now that I can't afford one.

A yawn sneaks up on me as I cross cursing off the list. I should try to get some sleep tonight since I am going into the

BA tomorrow. I add one last line—get the job at the bar—and then I tuck the paper into my pocket and curl up on the ground, moving until I find a position in the grass that will let me rest.

There are many noises I would prefer never wake up to, and the sound of shattering glass is in the top three on my list. Bloody murder screams and a chainsaw come in pretty damn close for first and second.

My head jerks up as more glass breaks. I wasn't even officially asleep and that noise is just as frightening. I survey my surroundings quickly as I sit up, wrapping my arms around my bent knees. The eerie quiet of the night and lack of life around me increases my heartbeat. I've sleep here numerous times, and this is the first I've felt as though my heart is going to pound out of my chest in fear before the murderer can find me and kill me off himself.

Shoot, why do I always have to think the extremes?

More glass breaks, followed by numerous loud thuds. I move to my feet quickly, pinning my back to the tree stump, and crossing my fingers that I blend in. More thuds sound from somewhere behind me and then the glass noise stops. Like an idiot, I peek around the tree. Two figures dressed in all black run out a door and pass under a street lamp in a flash before disappearing around a corner.

Oh my god. Oh my god. Oh my god. What do I do? Puke? Yes, I definitely feel something happening in my stomach right now.

I'm not sure how many minutes pass before I finally

release the breath I'm holding and step around the tree toward the doorway they came from.

Turn around, Sky; no good will come from you going over there. I take another step and stop. *But what if someone is inside and they're hurt and I'm the only person around?* Another step. *Or what if there are more than two intruders and the others are still inside just waiting for someone to show up?* I pause.

Of course I'm the only person out here in the middle of the night to do something about it. I choke back the fear.

I quicken my steps and when I reach the door, I find it still closed. There are two large windows on either side of the entrance. One window is completely broken out, which is why I'm crunching glass under my shoes.

The other window, the one that sits unbroken, has a bold white sign that reads Warren's Books. The hours are clearly visible below the name. *Why did they only break the glass on one side?* I poke my head inside; the register is in pieces on the floor near a counter and the shelves are either knocked over or in pieces, with books covering the floor. I lean in farther, making sure I scan every inch before coming to the conclusion it's safe to proceed, when I lose my balance and reach for the door to steady myself. A broken piece of glass sticking off the door slices open my palm. I jump back, clenching my hand.

"Holy mother—"

Footsteps. Someone is headed this way, and they're coming fast. Where can I go? If someone sees me standing here, they'll think I did this. Yeah, I don't have a job, a home, or even a place I have to be tomorrow, but I prefer having nothing to sitting in a jail cell.

. . .

Luke

The last thing I expect to find when I get to my family's store is the very same chick Beth was encouraging me to ask out standing in front of the door, broken glass on the ground beneath her.

"Hey! What do you think you're doing?" I yell, picking up the jogging pace I already had when I rounded the corner.

"I … I …" she stutters as her brows rise and her eyes begin to gloss over.

"What did you do?" I yell louder now that I'm standing in front of the store and can view all the damage she has done—including the broken cash machine. My reflex is to immediately grab her wrist.

"Give me the money!" I shout. My other hand is clenched. It's taken me this last year since my father passed away to get this place back up and running—even if we aren't bringing in more than we spend—and now all that hard work is ruined. No one is going to buy the place now.

"I didn't take it. I didn't do this." She stumbles over her words as tears fall from her eyes. "I heard it while I was sleeping." She attempts to pull her arm back, but I don't let up on my grip.

"Where were you sleeping?" There are apartments across the park, but I doubt she could hear anything all the way over there.

"I was …" She looks at the park across the street.

"That's right, you can't even think fast enough to make up an excuse," I snap. I don't even know how to act right now. This can't be happening. I shouldn't be mean to her. Then again, she did just destroy my bookstore. She doesn't deserve kindness.

"No, I didn't do it, because I was sleeping in the park!" she yells back, swiping the tears away with her free hand.

Dirt on her sweats and a grass stain on her heather gray hoodie.

She's homeless.

"Oh, that makes even more sense. A homeless girl breaks into my store for money so she doesn't have to sleep on the ground. Is that it?"

"No, that wasn't it at—"

"What, the money wasn't enough? You had to trash the place, too?" Some people will never learn the lesson of what hard work and dedication truly means. No, people like her want to take instead of earn.

The siren from a police car parking on the curb next to us causes her to jump. I take the moment of advantage and hold her by the shoulders in front of me with both hands. Blond hair pulled back into a high ponytail hits my face as her head drops forward. I flinch to get it out of my eyes and … whoa. Sweet ass. Sweats look good on her. Too bad she's a felon.

"Officer Maron," I say, redirecting my attention to my buddy Tyler's father, who used to catch us sneaking beers from his fridge when we were high school, as he gets out of his patrol car. "This girl did this," I nod back toward my store.

"And you saw her?" he asks, resting his hands on his hips.

"I saw her coming out of the store, yeah."

"I wasn't coming out of the store; I was turning around after I cut myself." She holds up her free hand and blood runs down her wrist. Officer Maron turns to get something out of his car, then returns to wrap a napkin over the blood.

"If you hadn't broken the glass, you wouldn't have cut yourself." How many lies will she make up to get out of this?

"Oh my gosh, I didn't break in!"

"The guilty always say that," I reply.

"Miss, what is your name?" Officer Maron asks.

"Skylar Atwood."

"All right, I need your ID."

"I don't have it."

I roll my eyes at her answer. Of course she doesn't. She's homeless.

"Address?"

"I don't have one."

"Phone number?"

She doesn't answer this time, and when Officer Maron looks up, she shakes her head.

"Can anyone confirm you weren't here during the time the vandalism took place?"

Again, she shakes her head.

Damn right, because she did it.

"I'm sorry, Miss Atwood, but I'm going to have to take you in for questioning."

She nods slowly, and I release my hold as she willingly steps toward the back of the cop car. She gets in and Officer Maron closes the door. Heated, green eyes stare at me from inside the backseat.

"Don't let her guilt trip you out of this. I saw her leaving. And why didn't you cuff her?"

"I like to make my job as easy as possible, Luke. Now why don't you call your mother and meet me at the station?"

"Why do I need to call my mom? I'm not in high school anymore."

"Is she still part owner of the store?" His left brow cocks up.

"Yeah."

"Then she needs to be there to help us determine which charges, if any apply. With no proof, we can't hold this girl responsible."

Another cruiser pulls up behind him. The officers step out and approach us.

"While you wait for your mom, these gentlemen will go inside with you to assess the damage."

I nod. He will do everything he can to make sure this thief is brought to justice. Once he pulls away, I follow the other two officers inside. I go for the money first, prying the cash drawer open and finding all the cash still there. My shoulders relax as I stuff the bills inside my pocket.

An hour later, I've discovered that nothing was stolen. How pointless—she didn't steal anything but my time. Only broken shelves and books thrown about. I can put most of the shelves back together with some nails and a hammer, and after a week, give or take how much time I have and how long a new window will take to come in, everything should be back in place and we can open again.

The officers wait as I nail broken boards to replace the front windows glass and then they give me a ride to the station. The damage might be minimal, but my family has been through enough this last year. We don't need some girl coming in destroying evidence of how far we have come. I'm going to make damn sure she has to pay for what she did.

CHAPTER THREE

Luke

The moment my mother steps out of the room after speaking with Officer Maron, I know from the look in her eyes that we aren't even close to being on the same page. In fact, she looks downright calm.

"Lucas, they don't have any reason to hold her."

"Yeah, they do. I saw her. How is that not enough?"

"If it were that easy to hold someone, our jail cells would be overflowing with people," Officer Maron adds. He gives his signature smile and nod to both of us before excusing himself.

I rub my eyes and comb my hands through my hair. All that damage and no one is going to be held responsible. The urge to punch something is strong, but following through with that feeling in a police station isn't a great idea. If they can't charge her, I won't get money from her to replace anything. I have no doubt the insurance company will sit in limbo waiting for answers before they cut a check. Without that money, I have to use my own, which I don't exactly have. Credits cards are becoming a dangerous part of my life.

My fists clench as I try to control my breathing.

I don't have time for people to mess things up. I can't handle any more curves life wants to throw me. I'm not even sure I'm handling it correctly now. I just want my life back. The easy one. The simple one. The *happy* one.

"Lucas—"

"I need some air."

I head for the door, but Mom's small hand over my shoulder stops me.

"I have an idea, but I don't think you will like it."

"Mom, I trust you. Do whatever it is you feel is best. I'll call you tomorrow," I say, exiting before she gets another word out. I'm in no place to make decisions for anyone else right now, and if I snap, I'd prefer for my mother to not be on the receiving end. She doesn't deserve it.

She also doesn't understand. Dad left me in charge. I'm the man of the family, and it's my responsibility to take care of everyone. He never said those exact words to me. He didn't have a chance to. But he didn't have to say them either. My family is important to me, and if Dad's death taught me anything, it's that we never know how much time we have left with the ones we love. Oh, and that drunk drivers take anything they want.

I walk faster, the cool air not doing anything to turn down the heat of anger in my gut. My family just can't catch a break.

I head for the BA where I left my car. If my plan to sleep above the bookstore wasn't a good idea before, it sure is now.

"Hey, man," Conner says as he steps out the back door

with Beth behind him. "Everything okay? We thought you were coming back a lot sooner than two hours later."

"Yeah, he made me wait an extra forty-five minutes to leave just in case something happened to you. Being a father and boyfriend has made him soft." Beth's tone is all for fun and she pretends to slug Conner's arm, but I can't bring myself to smile. Conner's girlfriend Alex becoming friends with that fugitive and bringing her into our lives probably led her to break into my store. If I hadn't shown up when I did, who knows what else she would have done?

"Wait, something *did* happen, didn't it?"

"Your little friend broke into the bookstore tonight. Place is completely trashed."

"What friend?"

"Cloud or whatever her name is," I answer, knowing full well her real name. I give them the short version, adding a glare for Beth since she is this chick's friend, too. It's not Beth's fault, but I need a place to channel my anger. I just can't help it. I've never been so mad in my life.

"Sky? Noooo, she wouldn't."

"She did."

"For real?" Conner asks, his voice showing just as much disbelief as Beth's.

"Yes. For real. Come by in the morning and see for yourself. I'll be there bright and early fixing the mess she made." I turn for my truck, then stop. "And don't bring her around me, all right? If I see her again, I won't be able to control anything that comes out of my mouth."

I slam my door shut and crank the engine. My tires squeal as I exit the lot and head home. Hopefully sleep will calm me down and help me think clearly. After all, I can still do everything I planned to do. It just might take me longer.

Skylar

One whole hour I've been watching the clock and answering the very few questions the detective has for me. He asked if I wanted a lawyer. It was a good joke. If I called one, my father would surely find out where I am, or worse, Mack would show up and scam me into going back with him. I'd rather be locked in jail than talk to my father or my ex-fiancé again.

Besides, I didn't do it, and I think everyone here knows it except that stupid, temperamental guy who claimed he owned the place and put his hands on me thinking I was going to make a run for it. *Only the guilty run, jackass.* The more I think about it, I'm certain he *is* one of Alex's boyfriend's buddies. This should go well.

"Well, Miss Atwood, we can't keep you here any longer. Thank you for being so patient with us."

I scoot my chair back as I stand. "A job's a job, right?" I say, faking a smile as I quote my father's favorite line and step around the table. I've wanted to burn that quote from my memory since the first time he said it to my mother.

"Before you go, the woman who owns the bookstore, Mrs. Warren, asked if she could have a word with you," the detective says quickly, since I'm basically darting for the door. I may be homeless, but that doesn't mean I want to stay here. Still, I stop.

"What for? I thought that guy from earlier owned it."

"He and his mother both do. Anyway, no one is forcing

you to talk with her, but I think you will like what she has to say."

Well, it's not like I need to be in a hurry to get back to my tree in the park.

"Sure," I answer, taking my seat again. The detective holds the door open for a small woman to enter and then closes the door behind him when he leaves.

Mrs. Warren is a petite blonde, maybe five foot three, who looks as though she could be in her early fifties. She's got jeans on with a baggy t-shirt and a light jacket. Her dark hair is pulled back, and she isn't wearing any makeup. She looks tired, which makes sense because it is nearing two in the morning.

"Hi." She waves, even though I'm the only person in the room. "Skylar, is it?"

"Yes, ma'am." I may choose to get away from a lot of things from my past and my family, but manners are something I'll never forget.

"I'm sorry for my son's behavior earlier. I've been informed of everything that happened, and I can assure you, he isn't normally like that."

I lick my lips and nod. There are so many things I want to say about her son, the first being she should never apologize for his behavior, but when she takes the seat across from me, leaning back with a yawn, I stop. She doesn't want to be here either. Why should I make it worse?

"He responded in a way I believe any person would have if they just found out their business had been broken into. I'm sorry, by the way. I wish I could have been closer to the faces of the people who did it."

"It was better that you weren't around. Safer. You never

know what a person is capable of. Which brings me to why I want to speak with you." She pauses, waiting for me to give her my full attention. "Officer Maron mentioned that there is a possibility you do not have a home."

My head jerks back at her bluntness. Just call me out for being homeless after your son attempts to send me to jail. Fantastic.

"I didn't mean to offend you," she says quickly. "I just, well, there is a vacant apartment above the bookstore that I thought you might be interested in, and, as you know, the bookstore will need some work, so hiring an extra hand would cut the delay in reopening."

"You want to hire me? After your kid just tried to have me thrown behind bars?"

"There are two sides to every story, and with no proof, I can't believe everything I am told."

Interesting.

"So you're just going to believe me over your own child?"

"I am going to believe in myself. A young woman needs my help, and I have a way to help her if she is willing to accept the help offered to her."

The air grows thick between us as I mull over her offer. A place to stay would be nice and a job, too. But this all sounds too easy—there has to be more to it.

"What's the catch?" I ask.

"Rent for the apartment will be paid from your hours put in at the bookstore."

"So, I won't actually be making money?"

"No, you'll have to get another job for that, but I can promise you that every night until you are ready, you will have a warm bed to come home to and a door with a lock to keep you safe."

Her voice catches as she focuses on her hands in her lap. A woman I don't even know is worried for my safety and has shown more emotion toward me in the last three minutes than my real mom ever did.

I need a place, and my heart won't let me leave here if I turn this lady down. I don't want to cause her more stress by doing that than if I had been the one to destroy her store.

"Okay."

Her head snaps up and she smiles.

"Okay," she repeats my answer.

She doesn't make any motion to move, so neither do I. However, I do break into a yawn that causes her to chuckle.

"Shall I give you a ride, then?" she asks.

I nod, covering my mouth until my yawn has passed. "That would be great. Thank you."

I follow her out of the room, and Officer Maron gives an approving nod as I pass him. Being in front of that store might have been the moment I needed all along to place me back on track to the new life I want.

CHAPTER FOUR

Luke

"Have you lost your mind?" I pace back and forth in front of my mother. Between losing my dad, the insurance not being enough to keep her on her feet, and now the vandalism, the stress must have gotten to her so badly she actually gave this criminal a job and a place to live with free access to the property she just tore apart. *Free.* We can't afford to give things for free right now. Mom knows this.

"Oh, I get it, joke's on me, right?" I stop pacing Mom's living room, giving her my full focus.

"Lucas, I've never seen this side of you. I don't like it," she says, eyeing me over the top of her book. "The last twenty-four hours you've been mean, and the tone in your voice is one I hope to never hear again."

"Mom." I sit next to her on the couch. "Someone broke into our store, and I know it was her. Even if—that's a big if —it wasn't her, how can you be so calm?"

"Luke, we've learned over the last year that accidents happen and there is nothing we can do about them."

"Right, but we can*not* go giving random people homes above the bookstore." Especially after I'd been planning to move in there. Another financial setback because of Skylar. Great. Just great.

"Lucas, she doesn't have anywhere else to go."

"Let her go back to the park." I slouch back into the cushion. That girl clearly has her own way of taking care of herself. She doesn't need my mother's help. I can't believe she even agreed to it.

"I've had enough of this rotten attitude. I won't say it again. I don't want to hear you talk this way, and you better start acting your age. Oh, and get to the store to help Sky, too."

"I have to help her? And you're already referring to her by a nickname." She's brainwashing my mother.

Mom shoots a fiery warning in my direction. I rise from the couch and walk backward toward the door.

"I love you, Mom, but this is the first idea of yours I do not support. One slip up and I kick her out, and that's not up for debate."

I twist to face the door before I can see her reaction. I let out a breath when I've closed my car door without hearing her call my name. All that and I still didn't get to talk to her about selling the store. Probably not the best time to bring it up anyway. I definitely didn't earn any son of year points just now, but I'm not planning on letting Skylar live there for very long either. She'll slip up, and when she does, I'll be right there holding the door for her.

* * *

I flip the switch and light illuminates the broken shelves, scattered books, and broken glass. Today everything looks worse than it did last night. It's like a twister tore the room.

I nudge a few books with my feet as I clear a new path inside the store. When I reach the back of the store, the glow of the light from the clock reads 9:17 a.m. My gaze drifts to the stairs to the apartment.

I bet she only took this as a way to ease her guilt. She got caught, and to keep up with her whole innocent appearance, she offered to help, making her come out looking like the golden kid all along. Not going to happen. If she's up to something, I'll be the first to figure it out.

"Holy shit, this place really does look bad." Conner and his girl, Alex, step inside. Alex's eyes are wide as she looks around with her lips in the shape of an O as Conner stuffs his hands in his pockets and frowns.

"This isn't even the worst part." I huff. "My mom is letting her sleep it off upstairs."

"Your mom is letting who sleep it off?" Alex is clearly confused. The look on Conner's face tells me he didn't tell her who did it.

"We can go over this as many times as you want, but I didn't do any of this." Skylar steps into the room. She's wearing the same clothes from last night, and her hair is frizzy as it's starting to fall out of the bunched up ball she has it in.

"I am so lost," Alex says.

"She did this," I inform her.

"I did *not* do this." Skylar crosses her arms.

"Did too."

"Oh my gosh, what are we, ten? Call the police department and ask them to remind you what happened."

"You called the police on her?" Alex gasps. "Are you okay?" She rushes to Skylar and hugs her.

"Is she okay?" I open my eyes so wide they feel like they are about to pop out of their sockets. "Look at my store!"

Skylar rolls her eyes at me before saying to Alex, "I'm fine. It was all a misunderstanding."

"Yeah, because you got away with it."

"Okay." Conner jerks his head toward the door. "Luke, can I talk to you a sec, outside?"

"I'm not going to leave her alone in here. Who knows what else she—"

"Oh for heaven's sake, I'll stay in here." Alex sighs right before winning a very short but intense glaring contest with me.

"Whatever." I follow behind Conner, leaving the door open so I can keep an eye on Skylar. My mom may trust her, but that doesn't mean I have to.

"Dude, this is insane. I thought you thought Skylar was hot. Remember that day we ran into them on the trail, when Alex still hated me? You said—"

"I know what I said. That was before I knew she had no respect for other people's belongings."

"You really think she did it?"

"She was standing right here." My hands go palm up. "In this very spot when I got off work last night. Who else could it be?"

"Bummer, I was really hoping we could do this double date and best friend couples thing."

"That's your concern right now?"

"Well, I sure don't think she did it. I'm sorry, man, but Sky doesn't seem like the type to break and enter."

"Well, I didn't think so either, but then again I didn't know she was homeless."

"Sky is *homeless*?"

His shocked expression confirms my suspicion: no one knew she was sleeping in the park. This may not have been the first time she's done something like this.

Skylar

"Tell me everything," Alex says. "How did you end up with Luke last night?" A half-grin appears on her lips.

Oh, this girl is confused.

"Not in the way you're hoping right now."

She frowns.

"If I tell you the truth, will you promise not to act different around me?"

"I'll promise to try," she says.

I open my mouth to get the next words out when I hear "homeless" practically yelled outside. Sounds like Luke wants to make sure everyone knows the worst of me. I better get my side out to at least one person before he makes me look worse than last night already has.

"I heard someone breaking in because I was sleeping in the park because I didn't have any money to stay in the motel again last night."

Her brows dip together.

"I have no money, and until Mrs. Warren offered me the room upstairs, I didn't have a place to live. Homeless, I believe, is what people call it."

Her arms wrap so hard and so tight around me, I fear for a moment my ribs might snap. When I grunt in an effort to catch my breath, she lets go.

"I always knew something was up. You couldn't seriously do yoga in the park every morning."

I laugh. "I've actually never done yoga in the park."

Alex forces a smile, but it doesn't last long. "Why didn't you tell anyone? Or at least me and Beth?"

I shrug. "I thought about it, but I still don't know what I'm going to do or where I'll end up, so I didn't want to keep track of a fake story."

"Yeah, but how did you become homeless?" Her hand slaps to her mouth the moment she says the last word. "I'm so sorry, that was totally out of line."

"It's okay. I just don't want many people to know, so if you promise to keep it between us, it might actually be nice to tell someone."

"All ears. I won't tell a soul."

"I'm from Seattle where my father is a very in-demand lawyer. Last I knew he was working on some kind of deal—I don't know specifics because, according to Maxwell Atwood, women aren't meant for the office. But the only way it would go through was if I married the son of the family he was negotiating with. I didn't want that, and my father told me if I didn't marry, he'd cut me off. So I left and here I am. Told the guy at the bus station to pick a place, and this is where it got me."

"Wow."

Not exactly the reaction I was going for when I revealed the summary version of my screwed up past, but it always shocks me when I think about it too, I guess.

"So, you have money, you just don't want it?"

"Not if I didn't earn it."

"Huh, that's interesting, and I think we should come back to this, but first, can I help you with anything? I still have some stuff in my brother's garage from when I moved out of my place and into Conner's. If you need furniture, you can have it."

I start nodding immediately. When Mrs. Warren brought me up here last night, I wasn't exactly disappointed to see only a bed and a closet with a few sets of sheets, but I really did think there would be at least a chair or a table.

"That would actually be great, but only until I can save up enough money to buy my own."

"Don't be silly, you—"

"Alex, I came here to start my own life by making my own way. This is definitely a bump in the road, but I can't take handouts from everyone."

She stares at me a moment, her lips popping out. "All right, you can pay me later for whatever you decide to use. So go shower and change and we can head to Logan's. He'll be so excited to have his garage back."

"Okay, I just need to go by the gym. That's where all my stuff is."

"You don't have anything with you?" she asks.

"Just what's in my backpack," I say. *Crud.* "It's fine. Please don't cry. Let's go."

"Go where? You're supposed to be cleaning this up. You know, the mess *you* made," Luke says as he steps back inside the store.

"Seriously, guy, let it go."

"It's Luke, not guy."

He crosses his arms in front of me as he plants his feet in the doorway. His arms are large and firm, and I can see the veins popping out of them. His brown shirt is caught on his belt, revealing that his jeans hang low on his hips in what I've always thought was the sexiest way.

"Luke, she needs to shower and change. Don't be so mean," Alex says behind me.

"I—" he begins.

"Just hurry back. I'll stay to help until we have to leave for class in an hour," Conner suggests.

"Fuck," Luke growls, his fingers practically pulling the hair off his head. "I forgot about class today."

"Actually, we need you to help us, Conner," Alex says quietly. "We're going to get some furniture from Logan's for Sky's new apartment, and you will probably have to do most of the lifting."

"No, no, no." Luke shakes his head. I don't miss the way his hands clench before they rest on his hips. "This takes top priority, and that apartment is temporary."

"That's not what your mom said." I cross my arms and mimic his stance. Luke's nostrils flare as his eyes never stray from mine.

"Luke, man," Conner steps up and puts a hand on his shoulder. "I'll still help you when I get back."

"Me too," Alex adds.

Luke's gaze doesn't soften. His eyes slowly move down my body and back up. The intensity radiating off of them actually makes me step back.

"We'll all go and get back sooner," he says to Conner.

"But what about class? I would like to help, but I'd also like to get this stupid degree before I turn fifty," Conner says.

"We'll get everything moved before class," he says to Conner and then points at me. "No more excuses to get out of taking responsibility for your actions."

"Yes, sir," I spit out, saluting him and walking through the door without letting him get in another word.

"Luke isn't normally like this." Alex rushes out behind me. "He's actually one of the kindest guys I know besides Conner."

"Could have fooled me," I say, avoiding eye contact with her. My heart is thumping loudly, and my fingers are beginning to shake. Luke's nailing every nerve I have with insults. I won't stand for it.

"I've also never seen him so worked up before." There is a hint of humor in her voice. "You must bring out a whole new side of him."

That makes two of us.

"The guy seriously thinks I vandalized his store. He can't speak to me this way forever. Today, yeah, he's still fuming off last night. I'll give him that. But sooner or later, he'll have to change his attitude. Especially when he figures out that it wasn't me."

"I agree. Let's make a plan to prove him wrong," she says.

"I don't have to prove anything to him."

"Okay, maybe not prove, but you could help him figure out who really did it, and perhaps you two could eventually be friends."

I stop, twisting to face her.

That's a brilliant idea.

I'm done allowing people use me or treat me like I'm not worth enough. I'm not taking the fall for the person who did this, and I damn well deserve to be treated with respect from

Luke. The friends part, though? I don't think that will ever happen.

I climb inside the back of Conner's truck as we wait for the guys to join us. Luke slams his door closed when he gets in and then glares at me though the rearview mirror. He doesn't speak the entire drive. Not even when Alex tries to include him in conversation. I want to kick the back of his chair like a little kid right now, but I also want to laugh because he is more worked up than anyone I have ever met.

I should remind him that he only gets one life, and I hope he chooses to not act like this forever. But then he glares at me again so I don't say a single word. I have more important things to worry about than what choices he makes in life. I have a vandal to find with no idea how to go about it.

CHAPTER FIVE

Skylar

The next morning, a ridiculous amount of banging echoes through the apartment as someone pounds on the door hard enough to make it fall off the hinges. I force myself out of bed —it turns out I've really, *really* been missing a decent bed and a night's sleep for a while now—dragging my feet until I reach the door. Since no one else in my life has the need to ruin such a delightful moment of the day for me, there's only one person this could be.

"What?"

"Um." Luke stands in front of me. His eyes go wide and he spins around. "You need to get dressed and come downstairs. We have a lot to do."

"You being my boss isn't part of the deal." I cross my arms and lean on the doorframe, fully aware I'm in a t-shirt and my panties. Yesterday, after we moved some new stuff into my apartment, Luke and Conner went to class at the local college. I convinced myself that his school schedule was going to allow me to work on the store alone. I apparently was wrong.

"I own this place; of course I'm your boss. No one should have to tell you that."

He makes a valid point, but no. I'm not taking it.

"Well, then you need to talk to me with respect, the way a real employer would."

"I think we passed the respect part of our relationship the moment you broke in."

I groan. "Still think I'm a criminal, huh? That sucks for you."

"Just get downstairs." He takes off down the steps, letting the door at the bottom slam closed behind him. Either slamming doors is his thing, or he doesn't know his own strength. Probably the former.

How much is this apartment worth to me? I mean, I'd almost prefer to be homeless again if it means I don't have to work with him. *Almost.*

After we'd moved the table and chair up here—there wasn't much room for anything else—Alex and Beth magically stopped by later with clothes they just had "lying around" or "were going to donate." At first I was embarrassed, but they insisted until I couldn't find it inside to say no anymore. I did need more clothes, and if I were going to take anything from anyone, it'd be those two.

I step into a torn pair of shorts, something I saw and immediately cheered because I could cross it off my list. The word *torn* has three underlines underneath it and is written in all capital letters. I've always wanted to wear something with a hole it. Anytime I've seen a girl with ripped anything, I always gotten this happy, carefree vibe from her. I convinced myself it was because they held enough confidence to wear the clothes they had, and I wanted that. There was a time or two I almost ripped a good pair of clothes just to make a hole. But I never could bring myself to do it. I didn't want to deal with my mother's cold stare. Just knowing I get to scratch this off the list now puts me in a cheery mood.

Turns out, these are my favorite pair of shorts, too. They are little short, but I don't care—I love them. Maybe that's because I can picture my father's eyes bursting if he saw me right now. And Mack—ha—if the public could see me now. I smile as I twist my hair up into a bun, sticking a pen through it to hold it up, and then put on a long-sleeved, white and yellow plaid fitted button-up. I want to go barefoot, but know there are still broken pieces of glass on the floor down there. I slide on a pair of flats and head for the door. There is no point in showering or putting on makeup because it's just Luke.

I do, however, spritz myself with the vanilla spray Alex gave me. She said she doesn't like it and wouldn't use it, but I think that was all a lie to get me to take it. Worked, too. It smells so heavenly, I'd have taken it with or without her excuse.

Once I brush my teeth, I head down the steps, chanting silently to myself to not roll my eyes at him. The guy says the stupidest things when it comes to this idea that I broke in, and he actually believes himself. He is wound up tight, this one. What's that saying? He probably just needs to get laid.

I find him walking across the room with a box of books. *Why, hello, biceps.* His flawlessly toned body and chiseled jawline are hard to deny. We may not get along, but he is freaking nice to look at. As of right now, this is the only perk of working with him.

"Are you going to help or just stand there and stare at me while I do all the work?"

"Well—"

"Just start moving those books to this corner while I work on piecing this shelf back together."

I salute him, which just causes him to groan in annoyance. *I feel the same way, jerk face.*

I grab a book then another. The cover isn't one I recognize, which, let's be honest, I don't know every single cover, but for some reason I find myself flipping it over to read who the author is.

Edgar Allen Poe.

I pick up another book by the same author.

"Who's the Poe fan?" I ask, turning toward Luke sitting with his board. His head snaps up and his eyes narrow when he spots the book in my hands.

"I said *those* books," he snaps, marching over, pointing at a different pile of books than the one I'm in front of and yanking *The Cask of Amontillado* out of my hand. I step back, watching and waiting as he grabs the remainder of the collection. He doesn't even look at me when he storms off, but it's all right. When he saw what I was holding, his eyes didn't narrow at me like they usually do. Instead they focused on the books like if he didn't grab them right away, he'd never get them back. I have the urge to ask him if he's okay, but my instincts tell me that wouldn't be the smartest move right now. Instead, I just head for the other pile and move the books in silence.

It takes me a while because I feel the need to alphabetize them as I move each one. Once I'm done, I look around the store space. It's one large room, aside from the door that reads restrooms. They have posters of upcoming releases on the wall, and judging by how they are placed, the posters serve as a guide to which books are in what section of the store. With a little makeover, this store could be a popular place.

"It would be really neat if you maybe made one of the back corners a reading nook. It's actually really common for book-stores to have a spot like that. Maybe even add a table or two and sell coffee. Or what if you had book signings? That would be cool. You could add some couches in different parts of the store, or those cute little round chairs in the corners so people can read parts of the book before they decide if they want to buy it. Or you could have some program where kids under a certain age can come in and read for free," I suggest, getting carried away with my vision. But Luke is on his phone. Texting, I assume, since the last few times I've looked at him, he's been looking down. He sighs and shoves the phone in his pocket. He must do it with more force than the ordinary person because it tugs on his jeans, revealing a glimpse of the spot just above his hipbone.

Yep, that area is toned, too.

"Buy furniture, add a coffee shop, and remodel every corner of the store? Do you hear yourself? If you focused on more than what you *think*, you'd know I'm not really in a place to redecorate. Most people don't just have money when-ever they need it. You of all people should understand that, right?" He dismisses my ideas fast. My heart races as I swallow and look away from him. I only wanted to do some-thing helpful, but he's right. I didn't think about money … I just assumed. "I've got to head out, think you can manage without me?" he asks. I try to hide my shock. He's leaving me alone. Here. *Finally.*

"And what do you want me to do?" I ask, since clearly anything I do will most likely piss him off.

"I don't care." He steps for the door. "Actually wait, that's a lie. I don't want you in here without me."

"That's going to be hard, don't you think, since I live up there and all." I point to the ceiling.

"Then you'll have to wait for me to get back."

"That's the first joke you've made the entire time I've known you."

He blinks, his face going blank. It reminds me of those guards' expressions, the ones outside the queen's palace who never smile, move, or speak.

"I'll be back in a couple of hours. Isn't there anything else you can do?"

I'm sure there is, but watching him freak out is the most fun I've had in days. Then again, I guess I could find something else on my list to cross off.

Luke nudges me through the door and locks it. He turns, ready to leave me standing there with no way into my apartment. I grab his wrist and then step in front of him.

"You can't seriously lock me out."

"I can do whatever I want. I own the place," he says.

"And I live upstairs." I take step toward him, my hands on my hips.

"You found a way in before; I'm sure you can do it again." With one step, he's towering over me. My eyes flash to his lips before they meet the dark irises staring down at me. His lips part, and for a moment my stomach clenches with the idea that he might kiss me. Which is silly, because it's obvious that's the last thing on his mind.

He takes a deep breath and steps back. "I'll be back in a couple hours."

And just like that, I'm alone, watching his backside.

Well, this is new. What do I do now?

The laughter that carries from the group of girls in the park across the street couldn't have had better timing. Alex and Beth. One of them will know what to do.

* * *

"He can't really think the only time you can be there is when he's there, can he?" Alex says, her eyes quickly looking away from my nails as she presses her lips together.

"Don't laugh at me," I say, not able to hold back a laugh myself.

"Okay, but I find it super hard to believe you've never painted your fingernails ever, *ever* in your entire life," she says, applying a clear coat of something over her new lime green nails. Which also happens to look like a professional did them instead of a two-year-old like mine. I'm no expert, but I'm pretty sure there should be more red polish on my nails than on the skin around them.

"Believe it. For a long time I accepted it and enjoyed being pampered."

"And one day you just changed your mind."

"One day I woke up with a guy next to me who I was supposed to love for the rest of my life, and, yeah, it occurred to me that I didn't love anything about him. That I would never see him as more than a guy who used to be my friend who had turned into a mini version of my father, and I wanted to be far away as I could be from everything that included him."

Alex blinks, not really giving away anything she's thinking.

"And now you come straight into a life with a guy who I have the feeling you want to be far away from also."

"It's not that I want to be far away from Luke; I just don't want to be around him. He's cranky and rude and can't listen worth a damn."

"Because if he had, he would understand you didn't do anything wrong and that you are an amazing woman."

"Yes, that." I laugh. "But maybe he would be nicer also and not put me in an argumentative mood every time I see him. I mean, come on, how in the heck am I supposed to go home if I can't be there without him?"

I'm not even going to mention that I thought about kissing him right after he locked me out. This, coincidentally, would have been the first time I wouldn't have argued with him.

"I have an idea, but you won't like it," Conner says, poking his head out from their room. He'd gone in there the moment I got here, saying he had to go over his new fall semester schedule and put some things together for Jake's school supply list. It must not have required too much focus if he knows enough to join our conversation.

"If it's going to annoy him, I'm sure I'll love it." I smile.

"You and Luke still aren't getting along, huh?" he asks.

"Nope, and I don't see that changing anytime soon."

Alex laughs, but Conner doesn't.

"What's your idea?" I say, twisting the cap onto my polish and dropping it into the bag with Alex's stickers, glitter, and more polish. I blow on my nails as I wait for him share his grand idea of how I can get into my apartment without Luke.

"You could call his mom," he says.

"Conner," Alex says, again trying not to smile.

"What? She is the only person he listens to these days." His nose wrinkles up. "Well, at least she was till she gave you the room above the store. Now he thinks she's lost her mind."

"I don't think this is a good idea," Alex says.

"And why not? I'll just call her and ask if she can get me a key so I can get into my apartment in the very real chance someone locks me out of the bookstore," I say. And also because maybe then I can get in and out without seeing Luke again and reliving whatever happened between us.

"And you won't say anything else?" Conner asks.

"Oh, now you're worried about it?" Alex asks him, rolling her eyes but still smiling.

"Once I said it, I realized what a bad idea it is."

"Why? It's just his mom."

Conner and Alex share a look. I don't want to let their reactions change my mind, because I need a key, and the only other person to ask who isn't Luke is his mother.

"Can I borrow one of your phones, please?" I ask.

"Better add that to your list," Alex says, grabbing Conner's phone off the counter with her fingers as wide as they can go so as to not smudge the paint and handing it to me.

"I don't know that I really need one here. Everywhere is within walking distance."

"At least look into it for safety reasons," Conner adds. "They have pay-as-you-go plans." He takes a seat on the sofa next to Alex and keeps his focus on me. He's so focused I bet if I flinched super-fast, he'd jump.

I turn away the moment she picks up.

"Conner, is everything okay?" she answers instead of the typical "hello!" greeting. I bet it does look weird that Conner would be calling her.

"Hi, Mrs. Warren, it's actually Skylar."

"Oh Sky, dear, it's so great to hear from you. How is the apartment so far?"

"It's great, and that is actually why I'm calling. It turns out that my key to the apartment doesn't let me into the store, and without getting into the store I can't exactly get to the apartment."

"Oh my, I can't believe I didn't think of that before. I'll be over this afternoon with a key for you."

"That would be fantastic, thank you." *Perfect idea, Conner.*

"How is everything else going?"

"So far, so good." It's basically the truth. Now, if she had asked how things with Luke were going, it would be a big lie.

"Oh that's great. Have you had a chance to buy food and things like that?"

"As soon as I get a job, I'll make it a priority to stock my fridge."

"I haven't seen you in two days. How have you been eating if you don't have anything in your fridge?" Her words come out fast, as though she is in a panic to say them. My mother never spoke to me that way. I've never been bothered by it before, but now I have an ache in my chest that I wish would go away just as fast as it showed up.

"Beth and Alex have been kind to me and brought me food."

"Oh good." The relief in her voice is hard to miss. I swallow, but it gets caught in my throat on the way down. My eyes start to feel wet; the last thing I want to do is cry. On the phone and in front of Alex and Conner, no less. I don't want them thinking I'm a homeless hot mess, even though I'm not homeless anymore.

"I'll see you this afternoon, Mrs. Warren. Thanks again."

"Please, call me Julie. I'll see you later. Good-bye, Sky."

I tap the red dot on the screen and hand Conner his phone.

I blink to dry the tears that want to fall at the pity expressions on their faces. I don't want their pity. I look away, spotting a newspaper sitting on that kitchen table.

"Can I take that?" I ask. "I need to start looking for a job."

"Yep, take it," Conner jumps up. "I have to get to class." He kisses Alex on the top of the head and grabs a notebook off the counter on his way out the door.

"Let's make list of the places for you to call," Alex suggests. "Do you have your résumé ready?"

"Um, no."

She laughs again and then pulls out a laptop.

"You should probably just go to the BA and talk to Sara. She'll give you a job," Conner says, returning to the bedroom.

"Not if Luke works there," I tell him.

Alex starts asking me questions of what I like, don't like, and what I know how to do. In just a few short hours, I have a résumé and a list of four places where I can drop it off.

I hug her when I leave, lucky as ever to have a friend like her. I also have more ambition for a job than I did before. Not only do I want to get away from Luke's angry attitude, but

I'm not sure I'm ready to have anyone treat me like his mother did, reminding me of everything I missed out in my childhood. I want to grow, not fall back into the unhappiness that was my life.

Luke

The door is closed by the time I make it to class, a clear sign that I'm late. After I left the store, I had to stop by the bank, since they wanted to go over the paperwork for the store now that there is a delay to sell. They graciously told me I will need to have an inspector sign off on the space before they can run their paperwork. I know it's just part of the process, but all I saw were dollar signs.

I knew that going over to the store this morning would put me behind, but we need to be working on it at all times, and fuck if I knew I was going to be waking Skylar up in a pair of damn skimpy panties.

All I wanted was a jump start on getting the place cleaned up before I ran my errands. Instead, I spent a solid hour trying to get the image of her half naked, with her perfect soft skin, messy hair and vanilla scent, out of my mind. I mean, come on, a thousand girls look like that in their underwear. But something was different. Her voice as she talked back to me was all confidence and temptation. No one ever argues with me, but two days with Skylar and she's tested my every nerve.

Then she had to go and stand in front me before I left, with eyes just screaming for me to kiss her. I almost did, too.

Fuck. What has gotten into me?

I step inside the classroom, thankful the door doesn't squeak at my entrance, and spot Conner in the front row. *He had to pick the front row.* We have English 101 together. A class we both should have taken by now, which is probably why we chose to take it over the summer. Fewer people. All summer exams are next week, and this one I'm actually stressing. Art I can do, but put words, real or not real, on paper and I have no idea what I'm doing.

"Mr. Warren," Professor Hend says, directing the entire class's attention toward me. Even in college, teachers love to point you out when you have done something they don't like. "This is the second day in a row you've chosen to arrive late to my class. Mr. Brian, at least, had the courtesy to show up on time today."

This is where I get lost. Should I respond because he stated a fact? It's true, so what does he expect me to say? Or does he even expect me to say anything?

"Well, what do you have to say for yourself?" he goes on, and damn it, I need to answer.

"Sorry" is all I can come up with. I have to so much to say and so much to argue, yet when I get here, I've got nothing. School isn't my problem right now.

I hear a few people chuckle, and gradually everyone returns their focus to the front of class. I take my seat next to Conner, who's failing to hide his smile behind his hand.

"I showed up on time and he still called me out for yesterday," he whispers. I just shake my head.

We make it through the next half hour without distraction, and finally Professor Hend dismisses us.

"Do you want to go shoot some hoops before work tonight?" Conner asks.

I wish I could. I miss lazy days of playing basketball all afternoon.

"I can't, man, sorry. I need to stop by the admissions office and drop some classes for this fall, and I should probably head back to the bookstore, see if I can get anything else done today."

Putting two classes on hold till next semester should give me the cash I need for the inspector and for the parts of the shelves I can't salvage.

"You're dropping classes?" he asks. We'd signed up for quite a few together. You know, the whole "if we're both there, maybe we'll actually get our assignments done" idea.

"Yeah, with the store, I don't think I'll have the time or focus for more classes." That's the first time I've admitted it out loud.

Conner stops walking once were outside the doors.

"Why do you put all the pressure on yourself?" he asks. "You have your whole life ahead of you and you're focused on taking care of a family who—don't punch me—already has a parent to take of them. Be young, man. Enjoy it and stop thinking you have to take care of everything. Your mom doesn't expect you do as much as you do."

Everything inside me is ready to burst. My mom doesn't have to tell me anything. She doesn't have to ask me anything. She's my mom. They are my sisters. I will do whatever I can to make sure they are safe and happy. They don't deserve to lose anything else. And if I just go about my life the way it was, well … I wasn't around much. I was always out with my friends, going on dates, or painting, pressing ignore on my family's calls until I finished with whatever I was doing. Everything I did before my dad died was on *my* schedule.

I have to be there now.

Of course, I don't say any of this to him. He cares, I know. But this isn't his life, and he doesn't get to decide which choices I make.

"Look, I have to go. I need to make sure Skylar didn't break into the store again since I locked her out, and we have a lot to do at the store today."

He releases a full breath and nods, his acceptance that we should change the subject.

"No worries—she's at my place looking for a job with Alex," he says.

"A job?" She can't have a job. If she gets a job, she won't have any time to work on the store and that would leave it all to me and I don't have time for that. She has to fix her mistake.

I shove past him and jog down the steps. I still need to stop by the administration office before I can get back to Skylar. The part of my life that is making everything even more difficult than my life already was.

"Hey man, I'll be at the gym if you change your mind about some hoops!" Conner shouts behind me.

For once, I just want one person to accept the choices I make.

CHAPTER SIX

Skylar

The feeling of fresh air and the sun warm against my skin is always a great way to put me in a good mood. And Lord knows after the last week I've had, I need it. Luke has been a royal dick ever since he returned to the store that day and I was already inside. His attitude makes helping out at the bookstore more difficult. Luckily, I have one job interview in a dentist office lined up, and hopefully, I'll hear something back on the other jobs soon. I gave them the number at the bookstore to contact me. That was a fun moment when Luke answered the phone and they asked for me.

I'd love to see Luke's face when he shows up at the bookstore this morning and I'm not there. Beth and Alex wanted to hit the trail at least one more time before the fall weather, and I didn't want to say no. I've needed a stress-free day like this.

"So, it's been a week. Are you and Luke getting along yet?"

"No," I answer Beth's question with no hesitation. We're

about halfway up the first hill and have already stopped for water and to catch our breath.

"And whose fault is that?" she asks.

"That's all Luke. I've tried, and I've not complained once no matter how bad I want to when he gets to ranting. He rambles so much. And that hand-brushing-through-the-hair thing he does when he gets really frustrated is so lame. But not as lame as when he balls up his fist so hard I think the veins in his arms are going to pop."

"So you like him and he's still a jerk. Don't you hate it when that happens?" Alex laughs and she leads us all up the hill a little farther.

"I don't like him."

"Yes, you do."

"Nope."

"I bet he'd be a lot nicer if you stopped acting ... hmm, what is the delicate way to put this? It's not immature, but more that you act like you're intentionally trying to piss him off," she says.

She's not too far off with that assumption. If he's going to be mad, I may as well make it worth it, right?

"He's still convinced I broke into the store."

"Did you?" Beth asks.

Alex stops, causing me to bump into her and Beth to push into me. *Why are we hiking so close together?*

"Beth, are you being serious?" Alex asks.

"Not really. I mean Luke is pretty convinced, though. I figure if she is going to admit it to anyone, it would be us."

"I didn't break into the store. I saw two people running away from it, I swear."

So much for a relaxing morning. I walk faster, my body

feeling warm as I try not to overreact to Beth's question, but it kind of pisses me off. I have two friends in this town and one of them might not believe me.

"Okay, well, what did these people look like?" Beth goes on.

"I didn't get a close look, but they were wearing all black and had on masks."

"That's like the typical robbery attire," she says through breaths behind me.

"Which means they are amateurs," I say.

"Why does it mean that?" Alex joins in.

"Because they couldn't be more creative?" It sounded a lot better when I said it in my head.

"That isn't going to work. What else do you have? Alex said you were going to look for these people, but what have you done?"

"Honestly, nothing. I don't even know where to begin looking. Unless two people wearing all black, both the exact same height and running exactly the same, were to walk up and offer to run down the sidewalk so I can place them at the store that night, I'm out of luck."

"What, like twins?"

At this rate, we'll never finish this hike.

"Yes, exactly like twins," I say.

"Did you know Luke has a set of younger twin sisters?"

"I did not know that; thanks for filling me in." I keep walking.

Would his sisters have a reason to do this? I would hope not.

"Maybe you were sleepy and saw the same person twice?" Beth asks.

"Nope, that wasn't it."

I stop again, since it's clear we can't talk and walk at the same time. "Beth, I'm not suggesting you need to pick a side, but I get the feeling that you believe Luke a little more than you believe me."

"It's not that I don't believe you, Sky. But it's Luke, I've known the guy for forever, and ever since his dad died, he hasn't been the same."

"His father died?" I ask, my voice raising slightly.

"Yes, and the store was his father's favorite thing in life other than his family."

I bet those Poe books were his dad's. *He misses his dad.* And that idea makes me sadder than thinking of my own father.

"Okay, well, I'll try to be nicer to him," I say.

"Don't give him the nice girl I'm sorry-your-dad-died pity act."

"It won't be," I say and look up the trail. Only three more miles to go.

"Are you ready to start now?" Alex asks.

"Not really," I laugh. "Why?"

The sounds of someone running fills my ears. From the smile on Alex's face, I know exactly who's running up behind us. *Please let me be wrong.*

I avoid eye contact, which is easy with the sun reflecting off his naked chest. His solid and smooth tanned chest. Things in the bookstore would get done faster if he looked like that at work. I try to find an interest in the rock next to my foot, but my eyes need another look. On second thought, I wouldn't get anything done if he showed up to work all sweaty like this.

"I have a feeling the only way I'll get any more work done

in the store is if I force you to stay there," Luke says as he and Conner jog up next to the three of us. "I was going to go easy on you if you actually did something before I got there. Guess that isn't the case today."

"Don't you have a life besides following me everywhere I go?" I ask, rolling my eyes and taking another step.

"This sounds familiar." Conner chuckles, pulling Alex in for a kiss.

Alex and Conner's story turned out way better than any relationship Luke and I will ever have.

"I'm not following you. You should be working."

"What? I'm not allowed one morning off? What are you doing—because it doesn't look like working."

"I'm not the one who—"

"I swear if you say trashed, broke into, or anything else that suggests I'm still to blame for this, I will slap you," I say, glaring at him.

"Maybe the two of you need to have a conversation that isn't about the bookstore—like, you both seem to like this trail. Skylar, do you like kayaking? Luke loves to kayak." Alex sounds so sweet as she tries to ease the tension the two of us have created on what was supposed to be a stress-relieving run. Complete backfire on both counts.

"I don't kayak anymore, but I see your point. Enjoy your hike, ladies. Skylar, please get to work when you're done here." Luke steps around us.

"You're not my—"

"I said please." His wide eyes focus on mine. I can't help that my eyes flash to his lips, again.

Damn.

I cross my arms, catching the questioning look on Beth's face. "Fine. And *please* stop cutting me off when I talk."

"Fine," he says, taking off at a sprint.

Conner hangs around for another moment, kissing Alex one last time before he follows Luke. I start back on the trail, stomping my feet. All conversations about Luke are over.

Please, *please* let me get one of these jobs.

Luke

"How's the store coming?" Conner asks.

It's just the two of us behind the bar tonight, which is a relief. I need an easy-going night.

"It'll be a lot better when the inspector shows up."

He told me it would be two weeks before he could come take a look at the store. What inspector takes that long? My stress level only increased that day, and lucky for Sky, she was the only one at the bookstore to enjoy it. Her version of that day, however, probably wouldn't include the word *enjoy*.

"All good things take time, right?" Conner squats to stock one the beer coolers. "What about Sky? How are things with her?"

"Let's just say, she is the last person I want to talk about."

Or think about any more than I already am.

One day. I try to trust her for *one day* because everyone says I need to give her a chance, and the day I do, she chooses to blow off work.

Speaking of which, I don't have a dress code at the store, but I am going to have to start. Short shorts and skirts and even those little flowy dress things she wears are not working for me. People should come into buy books, not be distracted by her appearance.

"You still think she did it?" Conner asks, pouring a pint of Bud from the tap.

"Yep," I tell him, because I do. But also because if I let myself think for even a second that she didn't do it, I don't know if I could trust myself to be alone with her.

"Okay, well, only because I'm ready for you to drop the sour mood and because I'd like for our group to hang out without the two of you bickering the entire time, I'm going to let you in on a piece of information that might change your mind."

I lean back on the bar and cross my arms. He's got my attention. All except for the small bit about me changing my mind. It's not going to happen.

"All right, so it turns out Sky's dad is some huge lawyer. She told Alex that her family was about to do a merger with another family that could lead to a large amount of money, and we Googled him and huge is an understatement. Like, her family is worth billions."

"She probably lied about that, too."

He shakes his head. "No, man, Sky is in so many photos with her family. Her mom is like some socialite who plans fundraisers and shit almost every weekend. There was even one article that talked about the mysterious absence of their daughter."

"They probably wrote it to hide the fact their kid is a criminal."

"Luke, seriously. She has money. Why did she need to break into your store, and if she did do it, she could just call her dad and get you money to fix everything."

"Which she hasn't done because it's all a lie. Don't let her fool you." *Who am I attempting to convince, him or me?*

"Well, she also told Alex that she left all that behind and is trying to make a name for herself."

"Such a shame the path she has chosen to go down." I won't budge. *She did it. She did it. She did it.* But she's so tiny, how could she have pushed those shelves down on her own? Or broken them, for that matter?

"Luke, man, she didn't do it."

"Okay, let's consider that you, everyone else, and my mother are right. That this is all just a misunderstanding on my end."

"Exactly."

"People don't just walk away from money, man."

"Sounds like Sky did."

"Fine, let's say it wasn't her. Who would you say the culprit is?"

"Honestly, it was probably just some high school kids trying to make noise or do what they thought was fun. You remember high school? We all did stupid shit."

"We didn't go around vandalizing."

"We egged your ex-girlfriend's house; I think that counts."

"Redecorating is not vandalism." I laugh.

"Right. But for real. You have to cool it. If I think you're being a dick, you're being a dick."

My head jerks back. Great, now I'm not just getting this speech from my mother. I saw Skylar standing there, in front of the store, with her hand cut from breaking the glass. I saw the fear on her face. No one else saw that. They don't get to decide this for me.

But … sigh. If everyone is going to tell me I'm overreacting, it's probably not a bad idea to reevaluate my situation. Even if I don't agree. "I'll talk to her," I say, referring to Skylar, but I'm really only saying it to end any conversation that includes her. He nods and walks away to make more drinks.

Neither of us wants to be around each other. Maybe I really should talk her. Mention the money. If her story is true, she won't have any problem getting the cash to find her own place or maybe to even donate to the financial loss I've taken because of her. Or, if her family is so easy to look up, maybe I'll just contact them and tell them just exactly what their daughter has been up to.

No, no. I can't do that to someone. I need the money and everything would be so much easier if it were handed to me, but that's not the way to go about it. I just need to keep working hard and things will eventually look up for me and my family. *All good things take time*, as Conner would say.

"Hello? Can we get drinks down here?" A brunette in a yellow dress slaps her hand on the counter to get my attention.

Fuck. I nod toward the woman.

My mind is all over the place. I have got to get rid of Skylar, especially now that the thought of her is distracting me from tips.

I make the woman's drink, spilling some of the vodka onto counter in the process. Once she pays me—minus a tip— I grab a rag and clean up my mess.

I never fully understood what people meant when they claimed someone was "driving them mad" until I met Skylar. I'm mad annoyed, mad frustrated, mad tired of her disagreeing with everything I say. I'm also just plain mad that I'm in the whole situation with her in the first place.

"Calm down there, friend. That spot looks pretty clean. You scrub it any harder, you'll have to explain to Sara why a section of her counter is missing its shine."

Beth's voice is calm, but I've known her long enough that there is more to it than the actual words.

"What's got you so worked up?"

Scratch that. This time she is saying the actual words.

"Nothing." I grunt it in a tone that Beth doesn't deserve. But, damn it, I'm not even around Skylar and I want to know what she's doing right now. Is she at the store? With Alex?

"I don't believe you. Now, no one else is around, so I suggest you either tell me what's up or I'll recruit Conner to help me get it out of you and then I'll tell Abby and you know how she—"

"Fine," I cut her off. I'd prefer if Abby, one of the other cocktail waitresses at the BA, didn't know anything about my business. She loves to meddle, and I don't need to add that to my stress level. She's been pretty low-key these last few months. I don't intend to bring the crazy back out in her.

Beth stops stacking the coaster bin, folding her arms as she leans against the counter. Her head tilts when she looks at me, waiting for me to speak.

"I was just thinking about the store and hoping that Skylar is doing what I asked her to do."

"You're thinking about Sky?" She grins.

"No, stop right there. Don't twist this like you girls do."

"I'm not twisting anything, Luke."

Her smile is even bigger now. *Great.*

"Okay, end of discussion." I step away, looking for the next piece of work to distract me, but sadly, no one needs me to make them a drink at this moment.

"No, it's not. Now why do you think she wouldn't be doing what you've asked her to do? I know the real Sky, and I bet she did exactly what you wanted. She's nice like that."

"I doubt that," I say. "She's probably destroying the place all over again as we speak."

"I doubt that," she says, mimicking my tone. "I know for a fact that is not happening."

"Any how do you know that?"

"Because she went to Alex and Conner's place to pick out an outfit for her upcoming interviews."

She isn't even there.

"Are you serious?"

"Okay, hold up." Beth squares her shoulders in front of me, her hands on her hips. "That girl had a whole life before this one. I don't know everything about it, but I do know she is trying to be a new person. And I also know getting a good, decent job is a big deal for her, so don't ruin this. It may even get her out of your hair every now and then."

Reopening my store and selling it is a big deal for me. She's going to ruin that by devoting her time to another job.

"If you ask me, a girl who's looking for a job isn't a criminal," Beth continues.

"Just walked by the bookstore." Logan chuckles as he walks in. "Place doesn't look like you've done a thing to it. Could it be that the two people putting it back together have been pre-occupied?" he asks.

"No," I say firmly and I hope it gets the point across that this conversation is over. That everyone knows this conversation is over. Especially now that I need to figure how to keep Skylar from getting a job. The store comes first. How do I make her see that?

Logan laughs again as he heads for the office. Beth joins him with a snort, and Conner smiles, punching something on the computer next to me. Why does everyone think I'm going to fall for this girl?

"Alex and I are having people over next weekend." Conner pauses. "Well, technically we're having people over at Logan and Sara's on account of the fact not everyone would enjoy being crammed into our little ole apartment, but the point is, you're invited."

"I don't think I'll be able to make it."

"Please, man. It'd be good to see you out. Even if it's only an hour," he says.

I could stay later at the store one night or go in early one morning. Or I could tell Skylar she needs to work more. I don't really have an hour of free time to spare, but every time I tell him I can't make it somewhere, Conner makes the same face his son does after he's been told no. I see that face at least three times a week.

"I'll be there," I say. *This week it'll only be twice.*

"Sky is invited, too," he says, looking in the opposite direction.

Of course she is.

I take a deep breath and nod. I know I need to get used to seeing her around because her friends are my friends, but that doesn't mean I have to like her. Thank god I have the BA as a getaway. I don't know what I would do if she became a part of every single place in my life. The bookstore is pushing it as it is.

"What's it for?" I ask.

"It's a surprise."

Everything with Conner and Alex is a surprise. It's like

they are always so afraid to just tell people something, they have to make it some huge thing when they do. My bet is on either he proposed or his sister Kelsey is pregnant. Again.

"I'm kidding, man. It's just a barbeque. With the summer coming to end here fast, we thought it'd be fun," he says.

"Sounds great. This time maybe we can finally win a quick game against Ethan and Logan."

"Dude, you know those two are together every day playing ball. We'll never win."

"That's not the attitude of a teammate I want to have. I'll just ask Beth to be on my team," I joke. Choosing someone else motivates him.

She laughs. "Then you will, for sure, lose."

"No, I got this." Conner loses any facial expression he had. "We can beat them."

"All right. All right."

Works every time.

The conversation quickly changes to talk of his son, Jake, Beth's brother coming to town, and how Conner hopes his classes are going to pan out. He's a semester away from graduating. *Lucky bastard.* I was a year away from graduating myself when my father died. Now I'm finding myself struggling to pass any class I'm in.

I need to get back on track, and I need to do it before the store falls apart and no one wants to buy it.

CHAPTER SEVEN

Luke

"No, you can't put those here." I nudge her out of my way with my hip. It's been more than a week and this place is no closer to opening. No thanks to the fact that the only new shelves I could afford are on back order. I had to call the inspector to reschedule for another week out. *Fan-fucking-tastic.*

"I'm sorry I'm not doing everything the Luke-approved way." The sarcasm in her voice is clear as water.

Skylar is another reason I'm ready to pull my hair out. I've never brought up her family, but I'll be damned if I don't want to scream at her. Every day we work together she sees me stress about how I'm going to keep this place afloat, and every day she doesn't mention a word. It's not like I expected her to come right out and say, "Luke, no worries, I have all the money in the world for you," but she—

Fuck, my issues with the store aren't her problem.

"You don't just toss books wherever you please. I have a system," I say.

She rolls her eyes at me, again. She does it every time I say something to her. Drives me up the wall. I wouldn't notice it so much if her eyes weren't so damn green and bright. It's just one of the many things that add to the fuel of my frustration with her. Being attracted to her is the last thing I need right now. And I can't seem to shake myself from stealing a glance every now and then.

"I didn't realize you had a system. Don't you think that's something you should have told me? You know, days ago? I bet things would get done sooner if we were on the same page."

"Things would have been done even sooner," I mimic her voice as best I can, "if someone hadn't done all this."

"Okay." She drops the book in her hand and glares at me. "I'm tired of listening to you whine about it. Since you are so darn convinced, why don't you tell me what motives I had for breaking into a bookstore of all places and not stealing any money or even a single book?"

"Because that was your plan, but I showed up."

"So, I just broke in, shoved some shelves down, tore them apart, broke as much glass as I could find, threw some books, and then came outside to take a break before I came back for the money?"

"Yeah."

"Do you even hear how stupid that sounds, Luke?"

I swallow and my head tilts back. She's never said my name before. I don't like that I like the way it sounds rolling off her lips.

"First timer and got scared." I shrug. "You were ready to

bail but then stopped and thought, 'I came this far, I'd may as well grab the money.'"

"Oh please, how did you even come up with that?"

"It makes sense." *Not really.* But I'm already committed to this assumption of the story. Can't take it back now and not look like an idiot.

"Yeah, about as much sense as you owning a bookstore." She bends down to pick up the novel that she dropped— it has a giant pink heart on the cover—and then grabs a few more romances and storms off in the other direction.

"Well, I'm glad to see the two of you getting along." Mom steps inside, leaving the door propped open so I can haul broken boards from the shelves I couldn't save out to the dumpster.

"Hi, Mrs. Warren," Skylar greets my mother before I can and in a sweet, soothing voice I've never heard before. *I don't like that either.* "He still doesn't care for me, but at least we're making progress on the store."

Mom's eyes meet mine, and I turn to grab a few more boards. Skylar's right, and if I were to argue right now, it would be in that tone Mom doesn't want to hear, so I may as well busy myself and not say a word. Once all the boards are out, I'll head to the bar earlier than I really need to be there.

I picked up an extra shift at the BA tonight, since I still don't know exactly when I can reopen the store. Bartending means I won't have anything to stress about. These days, all my stress is focused on the Warren's Books and little bit on the blonde whose silky smooth arm just brushed against mine. *Okay, maybe more than a little bit.*

"Sky, do you have plans tonight? I thought I'd invite you

over for an early dinner. Tonight I'm making cheese ravioli, Luke's favorite."

What the …

"Yeah, she's busy," I answer for her. Skylar and my mother, alone. Not happening.

"Actually," Skylar smirks at me and then faces my mother, "I'd love to join you for dinner, but I have plans tonight."

"Doing what?" I immediately regret asking the moment the words leave my mouth. I can't sound like I care, and that's exactly what I sounded like just now. *Think before you open your mouth, Luke.*

"I actually have plans with Alex," Skylar says. She glares at me and then turns to my mother. "In fact, I should get going to her place. Do you mind if I head out for the day?"

"Not at all. I hope you have a good time tonight," Mom answers.

"What?"

She can't leave now. There are still boards that need taken to the trash and books that need to be put in order so it's easier to place them when shelves come in, and the floor around the front counter needs swept and—

My mother shoots me a warning look and, damn it, even though I'm a grown man, she can shut me down in a heartbeat.

"All right, sure, go have *fun*," I say instead of arguing.

I can feel my mother's stare on me once Skylar is gone from the room.

"You need to learn to be nice to her. That girl is sweet and smart and funny. I don't think she could do something like this, and I've let you go on long enough."

"But she did break in, and why are you talking like the two of you are friends or something?"

She sighs. "Luke, I know you are convinced that because you saw her here, she did it, but that isn't the case in this situation. I need you to let it go. I don't want to hear about it again, and I'm sure I can speak for your friends in this matter, too."

It's like I'm back in high school.

"I don't need to be told what to do."

"Are you sure? Because your father was just as stubborn, and you're growing up to be the spitting image of the man, but that doesn't mean I want you to hold grudges like he did."

I give my attention to the James Patterson poster on wall instead of to my mother. Dad held a grudge for everything. Even the smallest thing, like me hitting a baseball through the basement window. Years later he told me I could have had a nicer car the day I turned sixteen if he hadn't had to spend so much money fixing the window, the wall, and the TV that the ball went through. I know it couldn't have cost that much, but that's not the point. He never let anything go, and I hated hearing him tell the stories of my screw-ups over and over.

"That, and it was your father's request that if your life suffers in any way by owning this store, I am to suspend joint ownership."

"My life isn't suffering," I tell her.

It may not be where I thought it would be, but I'm not suffering.

"Luke. I won't stand by and watch you act this way toward that girl or miss out on having fun in life, all for the sake of this store."

This is total bullshit. It's like she's telling me everything I've done isn't worth it.

"Fine, I'll work on it," I grit through my teeth.

"Promise me."

"I promise."

She rubs my back instead of giving me a hug before she leaves. I stay for another hour and a half. I don't get much done by myself.

And I couldn't help but notice, Skylar never did come back down the stairs to go to Alex's place. Why did she lie to my mom, of all people? Great, another reason to not like her. Unfortunately, I can't sell the store if I'm not joint owner and I can't stay joint owner without being nice to her. Then again, no one said I had to mean it. I could fake being nice. How hard could it be?

Skylar

Alex gave me a nice dress with sandals and a cardigan to wear for my interview today. I already had it, so I didn't really have to go to her place last night, but I didn't want his mother to have to witness the argumentative mess that is me and Luke. She deserves better, but that meal sounded amazing, and a part of me was tempted to just show up for dinner.

I push the door open and hold my head high. My first interview is for a receptionist position at a dental office. Answer phones and make appointments. I don't have experience, but I have a drive, and that counts for something.

I really want this job. I need to get away from Luke. Everyone keeps telling me about this totally different person. A guy who is funny, sweet, and kind. One who has manners and knows exactly how to get the girls to fall for him. His physical appearance makes me believe it, but when we talk, all I see is a man who is stressed, conflicted, and unhappy. If I'm the only person everyone is trying to convince that he is a good guy, then that can mean only one thing: I'm the reason he is unhappy and stressed. And as much as I would love, *love, love* to stick around to show him how wrong he is, I can't. I lived too long with people who made me unhappy; I don't want to be that person to anyone, ever. Not if I can help it anyway. I have four interviews over the next three days. I'm bound to get one of them. Then I'll move out.

"Hi," I say, smiling at the woman behind the counter. She smirks and goes back to what she was doing. "I'm here for an interview."

"Have a seat." She doesn't look up.

This must be why they are hiring. I may not have experience, but I have manners.

I sit, as she told me to do, and I wait. I wait ten minutes. Then I wait ten more. When thirty minutes pass—because I don't know how long I should wait for something like this—I return my attention to the girl behind the counter.

"Me again." I smile and try to laugh. "I just want to make sure I had the right time for my interview?"

"You did, but it turns out, we just filled the position. I'm so sorry for your trouble."

"Oh, I see." I pause. How did they fill it if I'm the only person who has been waiting? "Well, thank you for letting me know." I turn for the door when she doesn't respond and walk back out into the warm air of the afternoon. So my first interview didn't go very well or even at all. I'm sure this has happened to everyone at some point. Maybe not getting this job is a sign that I'm meant to have another position.

* * *

"We are so terribly sorry to have you come all this way, but we filled the position yesterday."

I smile and nod, just like I did at the dental office and leave the way I came. So, two jobs so far haven't worked out. I still have two more. I haven't lost hope.

But it is strange that they seemed happy to have me come in on the phone and now, I don't even get a two-minute chance to tell them this would be a great for me. Something doesn't add up. Is it because I put the bookstore for a phone number? Maybe that turned them away.

I head back toward my apartment by foot. I could easily go to the BA, the way Alex and Beth keep telling me to, and get a job, but that would defeat the purpose of getting out of Luke's way. A small part of me wants to yell *who cares?* and tell him to get over it. But I want to move on, too, and I don't want someone holding their stupid accusations of me breaking into their bookstore over my head.

I stop.

Could they know? Would Luke stoop that low? I mean, he wants me gone, right?

* * *

After the third interviewer informed me that they had already filled the opening, I started to suspect something, but this, this fourth rejection, just screams that something is going on. I might not have a lot of experience, but to not get any of the jobs—it's not just me.

"Again, I am so sorry you came in here today only for us to inform you that we offered the position to another person first thing this morning."

"I understand," I tell her in my cheeriest voice. "Thank you."

I turn for the door.

"Such a shame when you work so hard for something and someone just takes it all away. Poof, it's gone," she says with my back still facing her.

Bingo. *Luke*.

My teeth grind together under my tight-lipped smile. *I knew he had something to do with this.* I shove the door open and with heavy steps, head for the store.

I'm only a few blocks away, picking up the pace as I get closer. The clock in that office read two thirty; Luke will be out of class by three. I hate that I know his schedule. He'll come by the store to make sure I'm working before he heads to the BA, and I'll be there waiting for him. I have a half hour to come up with words of fury.

I round the corner, a couple blocks from the store, when a man placing a Volunteers Needed sign in the window catches my attention. The second thing I notice is the small, yellow Lab puppy under his arm. He disappears from the window that I'm still standing in front of. I search the window for a name—Mrs. Mulligan's Pet Care in small letters at the bottom.

It's not a paying job, but my parents never let me have a dog, which is why "get a dog" is on my list. Until I get a place that allows pets, this is as close as I'm going to get. Playing with puppies is exactly what I need right now. There is also a good chance Luke won't have gotten to them before I walk in here right now.

The bell over the door chimes as I push it open. It's loud in the quiet waiting area and immediately I hear musical barking come from the back room.

"Damn it, I have got to remove that bell," says a man as he comes through the back room door. He couldn't be much older than my age, with jet black hair that shines from all the gel under the light. His eyes look almost as dark as they settle on me.

"Can I help you?" he asks.

I stand straight and nod. "Yes, I want to volunteer or, if possible, apply for a job."

The left side of his mouth twitches up as he leans onto his forearms on the counter in front of me. "Well, we aren't hiring, but we are accepting volunteers. My little brother usually does the job, but he's got a lot going on with school, so I'm filling in for him, but I can't seem to get his job done on my own." He chuckles and I find myself smiling back.

"Are you the one who gets to make those decisions? I mean, about bringing in more help."

"No, but I can almost guarantee it's going to be okay. Come on back," he says, waving me to follow.

"Oh, I can start now?"

"Yeah, but don't wear white pants next time because they will be dirty in the first thirty minutes."

We step through a door that leads to a hallway of cages. It's just the way I imaged from the movies. Kennels line each side of us, and almost each one has one pet inside.

"We keep the cats in a separate room." He pushes open

another door, showing all the cats. "These are the two rooms you'll most likely be in. But before that, I should show you what you can do to help. Let's go meet Mrs. Mulligan. She's owned this place for as long as I can remember."

He knocks on a door and opens it before anyone can answer from the other side.

"Hey, Rose, this is ..." The guy pauses, waiting for me to fill in his sentence with my name.

"I'm Skylar, and you are?" I ask.

"Cory." He flashes me a grin that warms my cheeks.

"Cory, stop flirting with all the ladies. That gets you and your brother in more trouble than either of you need." Mrs. Mulligan says.

"Yes, ma'am," he says, although he's laughing, so I'm not sure any of what I just witnessed was real. "Skylar is here for the volunteer position."

"Come in, dear, let's have a chat." She points to the chair next to her.

I get right to it. "I've never had a pet before, but I want one. I also am pretty sure I can't have one where I'm living, but that's okay because I don't even know how to take care of a pet, so I thought maybe if I volunteered here, I could learn."

Her brows dip together and she leans back in her chair.

"You don't know how to take care of an animal? How old are you?" she asks.

"I know the basics," I answer, because I'm pretty sure I do. You feed them, bathe them, and let them out to us the bathroom and stuff. Of course, you give them endless love, too, but what about shots and appointments and how do I know what food to give them and is it bad to give them treats all day?

"Call me crazy—" Rose begins.

"We all do," Cory cuts her off from the doorway.

Rose throws a tennis ball at him. I can hear his laughter all the way down the hall.

"Call me crazy," Rose continues, "but I'm going to give you a chance."

"That's it? No more questions? What if I'm a murderer or something?" The moment the words are out of my mouth I wish I could take them back. *Way to go Sky—the one chance to get away from Luke and you blow it.*

"Are you a murderer?" she asks.

"No."

"Than that settles it." She stands with her hand in front of her. I do the same. "You remind me of someone I know. If you're anything like her, you will be perfect for this job." She shakes my hand and then points to the doorway. "I'm surprised you aren't looking for a paying job. That apartment can't have much in it, what with it being vacant for years."

I freeze the moment I'm standing again. "You know who I am?"

"Why, yes, dear. Luke hasn't shut up about you since you shattered the glass into his life."

I try not to smile. That's the first I've ever heard it put like that.

"Of course, he isn't saying the nicest things right now, but all boys are mean when they like a girl. It's how we humans work."

"I don't think that's the case with me and Luke."

She hands me a few papers and a pen. "You can sit back down; we may as well fill out these papers now and you can start tomorrow. Don't want to get your pretty outfit all dirty."

"I can start today. I don't have anything else going on."

"So you aren't out for interviews?"

Who is this lady?

"I hear everything in this town, and, dear, if you want a job, you should look to your friends at the bar. They are the best part of life."

I laugh. "If you hear everything, you must know that Luke works at the BA, so me going there isn't the best idea."

"Well, he did tell everyone he could that you were the girl who broke into his store—which, if anyone listens to gossip like I do, they know that isn't the case. I don't think you'll have much luck finding a job elsewhere. I'd say it would serve him right."

"What would?"

"He clearly doesn't want you getting a job, so why not get one at the place he works? Don't let his actions keep you from getting what you want. Karma sucks, my dear. That boy needs to be put back in line, and you're just the woman to do it."

I start filling out my paperwork, allowing her words to sink in. She's right. I can't let him get in my way, and a job is the first step to getting everything I want. The moment I leave here, I'm heading straight for the BA.

CHAPTER EIGHT

Luke

"Are things improving with you and Sky?" Mom asks over the phone. I called her on my way in to work tonight to see if she needs anything. I was implying food, money, that kind of thing, and maybe to bring up her signing over her half of the store, again.

"It's great," I lie with a big smile. I mean it's not *bad*. *Per se*.

"Hmmm." The disbelief is crystal clear though the speaker.

"Hey, so before I forget," I attempt a smooth transition to the more important subject. "Signing your half over could mean—"

"Oh Luke, you are always so focused on work. It's time for you to live a little. Go out."

"I go out," I say.

"Mmm hmm." *Is she distracted?*

"I do. I'm actually going to Conner and Alex's barbeque this weekend."

"Huh."

"With Skylar, we're actually going together," I lie. This isn't good. I keep lying to my mother. But she seems to only want to chat these days if it's about me and Skylar. And I need Mom to talk if she is going to sign over her half.

"You are?" I can hear her smile.

"Yeah, I'm picking her up and everything."

"Oh, that's fantastic." She cheers, and if I've heard right, sighs into the phone. "You better get to work. I'm really happy to hear things are already getting better. I knew you would come around."

She clicks off the line, leaving me to sit in my car trying to understand the phone call. Skylar must be my key to full ownership right now. Hopefully, Skylar will be just as easy to please as my mother was. There's only one way to find out.

Looks like I'm inviting her to ride with me this weekend.

I know I'm not the first one to arrive to the BA because Conner's, Sara's, and Logan's vehicles are here.

Sara and Logan own the bar, and Logan occasionally works here, but Sara never does now that they have a baby at home. Her being here is more than likely one of two things: someone is being let go—highly unlikely since we are a close group—or they are hiring someone new.

The idea is great, but sharing shifts and tips doesn't sound like a good idea to me.

I enter through the back door on the side with the parking lot and head up front. Conner's and Logan's voices carry from the back room as I pass. I'm almost to the front when a female tone I'm growing too familiar with fills my ears.

"I've never actually made a drink for anyone before, but I'm a quick learner."

No, no, no. Not here, too.

"Have you ever waited on anyone?" Sara asks.

"Just at the diner next door."

"All right, well, Conner and Alex have both said great things about you, so how about we get some paperwork done and put you on the schedule? In a couple of weeks, we can review and see how things are working out."

"That sounds great," Skylar replies.

I step into the open bar, and when Sara looks up at me, she smiles. Skylar has her back to me, sitting at the bar top.

"Oh, Luke, this is perfect. Since you two already know each other, I'm going to have you train her for the next two weeks. You don't mind, do you?"

Tips definitely just went down and so did my mood. Not that it wasn't already pretty low. The bookstore, here, and pretending we are great friends. I'm about to get in way over my head.

Blond hair flips over her shoulder, and I swear I'm in a movie watching how slowly Skylar turns to face me. Bright, hopeful eyes meet mine, and her lips part. Instead of saying anything, she gasps lightly, and I sure as shit hope I didn't just do the same.

My eyes immediately fall to a set of plump lips before finding her eyes again. It's as though my entire body forgot how to do anything but stare. I've never seen her look like this before. I mean it's her, but it's nice. She looks … I can't pull my eyes away.

Skylar looks nervous, and when she licks her lips and

swallows, I try my best to look at anything else in the bar, but I can't.

Sara clears her throat and bumps Skylar. She blinks, the moment gone. Skylar turns her gaze down to her hands, but not before I catch the faint pink of her cheeks.

"I'm just going to grab you a couple of shirts and a few other things from the office. I'll be right back," Sara says, sliding off her stool and leaving me alone with Skylar.

"So, you got a job. Here, of all places." I step behind the counter and punch my employee number into a computer to clock in.

"Well, you did make it hard for me to find one anywhere else." Her tight-lipped smile is a dead giveaway that she isn't pleased with me. Right now, I need her to like me and my company.

"I'm sorry. I shouldn't have told people not to hire you. I was holding a grudge, and I made poor choices on how to handle it." The words come out too easily; I'm feeling just as shocked as she looks. "I was hoping I could make it up to you by taking you to Alex and Conner's barbeque this weekend. I could pick you up from the store."

Her mouth opens and her eyes grow even wider than before. Her delayed response starts to worry me. I take a deep breath and wait. She's still looking at me. Still silent.

"You're forgiven, but I'm riding with Beth," she says.

This time it's me who doesn't say anything. I nod and then walk away. Why does it bother me she said no? It's like I was asking her out for real. Was I?

CHAPTER NINE

Skylar

I'm not so sure going to a barbeque with all of Luke's friends is such a good idea. I tried to use the rainy day as an excuse. People don't have barbeques in the rain. It just makes sense not to, but in this town, they make it work, and they get together no matter the weather.

The wind is howling, and the rain pelts against the windows. Thunder strikes and the lights flicker.

I should really stay home. I have no idea what happened at the bar a couple of days ago. I think, *I think,* Luke asked me out. Something about it … I don't know. It just came to him so easily, like either he had rehearsed it or maybe he actually meant it. Either option stirs my stomach. Say he did rehearse. That means it's something he didn't really want to say, which is annoying, but then why would he say it? And if he did mean … yeah, I don't even know where to start with that one, because that would be super out of the blue if Luke one day magically decided he liked me not just as a person but enough to take on a date.

"Hey girl." Beth walks into my apartment as if she lives here, too. "Are you ready?"

She's completely dry. I wrinkle my brows as I take in her appearance and then look out the window.

"How are you not soaking wet?"

"Well, we have this handy dandy thing called an umbrella." She laughs, showcasing the black stick in her hand. She taps it against the ground and the edges flair open. So much for another attempt at not going. Not that I had another excuse.

"I can't believe everyone you know is still going to this thing."

"Well, not everyone. Abby caught a cold, so she isn't going."

A cold. That would have been an easy one.

I could say I don't want to go, but that would be a lie. I simply don't want to run into Luke, because now I'm not sure if I need to act like we always do and argue, or if I should be nice to him. This should be an easy decision, and I hate that I have no idea why I can't decide.

"Today, girl. I'm going to have white hair by the time you get that coat buttoned."

I snap out of the new Luke daze I've let myself fall into. I've actually fallen into it quite a few times since he invited me to go with him, but no one needs to know that.

I grab my purse, placing the strap across my body, and follow Beth down the stairs. I lock the door and huddle under her umbrella with her till we reach her car.

"I know I don't have to tell you this, but just in case I do, I'm going to anyway," Beth says, buckling her seat belt.

"Okay …"

"You and Luke need to be nice to each other today. There will be kids around."

I laugh. "Yes, I assumed that was the role we would take on today."

"I mean it. And I hope you're going to be nice to each other when you start working at the bar, too. We are there to make money, and all other emotions should be set aside."

"Beth, is something bothering you?"

"I just really wish the two of you would get along. He's one of my oldest friends and you're one of my newest. I'm tired of being the middle man, and I don't want to have to choose."

Darn. I didn't realize we were that bad. I mean, I guess I did know. But I didn't know it was affecting Beth.

"I'll try harder. I swear."

"Really?"

"Yes, but can I ask you something without you getting upset?"

"Um, I can't make any promises."

"All right, well, you seem to consider Luke's feelings a lot." I hesitate, unsure if I want to know the answer. "Do you think you might have feelings for him?"

She laughs. "I can assure you I don't. I've just known him for a long time. He's a good friend. I swear. That's all it is."

"Okay." I lean back in my seat, pinching my lips together to keep from smiling as I watch the raindrops glide down the window.

"Would that bother you?" she asks. I twist to look at her.

"No. Not at all." *Was that too obvious, too quick of an answer?*

"Are you sure?" A sly smile starts to appear.

"Why does everyone think I should date Luke?" I ask. Maybe her answer will help me think clearer.

"Because all of us had already matched you two up in our minds before someone broke into the store."

"So you don't think I did it?"

She sighs. "I never thought you did. I shouldn't have said anything that day we were hiking. I'm sorry. No one believes you did anything."

Except Luke.

"I think Luke may have asked me out," I tell her out of nowhere.

Luckily, Beth was already slowing to stop being a long line of cars parked on a neighborhood sidewalk. Her car jerks to a halt at the same time I notice that the layout of each house is almost exactly the same as the ones next to it. It's like a neighborhood of cloned homes.

"Warn me next time you attempt whiplash," I say, observing her hand until she's put the vehicle in park and I can safely take my seatbelt off.

"When were you going to tell me he asked you out?"

"I didn't think it mattered. It was a couple days ago. He asked if he could pick me to come to this thing."

"What? Just yesterday you asked me for a ride. Why did you do that?"

That's a very good question. *Why did I do that?*

"I couldn't say yes just because it was the first nice gesture he made to me. Twenty-four hours before that, he was shouting at me about how I was doing everything wrong and he was telling the entire town not to hire me. It was weird. I went with my gut and said no."

"This is huge. Oh man, this means things are good and we can all be normal now."

She climbs out of the car, again with her umbrella, and comes to my side. I duck under the cover as we speed walk to the house.

"This is not normal," I tell her. "Don't you think it's weird he would do that?"

"No, I've been talking you up since the day I met you. It's about damn time."

Beth shoves me inside the house before I can reply. I'm in mid argument when the crowd makes me stop. Kids run past me, screaming as they chase each other, and people of all ages are grouped up, chatting away. There have to be at least thirty people in my view from the front door.

"They really go all out when they have people over. Plus, everyone is everyone's family, so it's hard not to," Beth says.

"You mean you're all related?"

"Well I'm not and Luke isn't. But Kelsey and Conner are brother and sister. Logan and Alex are brother and sister. Kelsey married Ethan, who is cousins with Sara, and Sara and Logan are married. And then you know how Conner and Alex got together."

"Right, yes, that was a good time." I laugh. "What about Abby?"

"Abby is not related to anyone. That's probably for the best, too."

"Oh, are you all not friends anymore?"

"We should have cut her off years ago, but somehow we still care about her no matter how many poor choices she makes. She's been pretty low-key lately though. It's been nice."

"Beth, Sky, over here." Alex waves us to where she, Sara, and Kelsey are standing. As we shrug off our coats, hanging them in the coat closet near the door, goose bumps prickle my skin. Someone is watching me. I turn to scan the room and … I was right. Luke is watching me from where he's sitting on the sofa. A smile twitches on his lips when we lock eyes. He nods and holds up his can of Pepsi to me in greeting.

I nod fast, and take off after Beth.

I told her I would try to make things between me and Luke better. Nothing can fix that better than a truce of some kind. I hope he sees it the way I do.

Luke

It was as though every part of my body knew she had walked through that door. Mind, heart, stomach, eyes, *and* groin. She didn't notice me right away. Which is good. I needed that moment to decide what I should do next and how I feel about whatever I choose to do.

My mother wants me to get along with her. I want to get along with my mother. I made the first effort to be friends with Skylar, and she turned me down. How could she turn me down? It was my store that she—*fuck,* I really have to let that go. That isn't even what I'm most annoyed about right now. I'm annoyed she said no, damn it. I hate that it bothers me, and I hate that it's taking all I have to remain sitting on this couch instead of going to find her. That's another thing that annoys me. Any time I'm around her, it takes all I have to do anything.

"You're supposed to be having fun." Conner takes the seat next to me. Jake runs up behind him, struggling with the zipper of his jacket. Conner zips it up and then tightens the strings around his hood. Jake jerks back.

"Dad, don't do that."

"You need to bundle up."

"I don't want it on."

"It's on, or you're staying inside." The father voice comes out thick. Jake runs away, his hood still covering his head.

"You're letting him go outside in this weather? After we called off our rematch basketball game because even we don't want to be outside in this downpour?"

"It wasn't really my choice. Logan bet Jake and Claire an extra scoop of ice cream that he could run faster than them around the back yard, even if it's raining. Once he planted the idea, it was hard to change their minds."

Loud screams and squeals fill the house. Conner jumps, and I turn quickly to see Logan chasing the kids out the door.

Alex is shaking her head with a laugh, watching them through the back window. She pivots on her heel, coming to a pause. She smiles at Conner, and a crimson color sweeps over her cheeks.

"Isn't she beautiful? I still can't believe she's mine," he says.

I'm nodding when Skylar comes into view behind Alex. Her eyes lock on mine.

"Yeah, she sure is something," I say.

I twist back around and look for something else to focus on. I can't like her. This is so freaking out of the blue. I despise her.

I release a loud breath, glancing up to come face to face

with Beth. She's sitting on the end of the coffee table with a knowing grin.

"So, what's this I hear you asked Sky out?"

"She told you about that?" *What did she say?*

"Well, don't you sound hopeful."

"You did?" Conner asks, his voice a little high with excitement.

"I just asked her if she needed a ride."

Right then, my ears are filled with cries of a small child. Logan is walking in the back door with Claire hugging him close as he carries her. Jake looks bummed out. Conner rises from the couch, leaving me alone with Beth. This is good. If I tell anyone the truth to figure out what to do, it's Beth.

"I think I made a mistake," I whisper just enough so no one can hear us but firm enough that Beth leans in.

"What did you do?" she asks.

I survey the room to make sure no one is near.

"My mom said she is going to take my half of the store away if I don't get my shit together. She kept implying my attitude with Skylar, so I sort of made it sound like we are on better terms than we actually are, and then I asked her out, for show of course." *I think.* "But now I don't know. I feel weird about it."

Beth is glaring and then punches me in the arm. I flinch from the fact I wasn't expecting that.

"You fake asked her out?"

Okay, maybe Beth wasn't the right person to tell.

"Well, I really would have driven her here."

"Under false pretenses. God, Luke, here I had hoped you were finally turning around, and you were only pretending. Why?"

She starts to rise, but I grab her arms, gently asking her to sit back down. She does.

"All right, so I've been a jackass. But why do you think she said no?"

She's shaking her head when she crosses her arms. "Sadly, I don't have that answer for you. But why don't you ask Sky what she thinks?"

"Ask her why she turned me down? I can't do that. That would imply I actually care when it was only a pity invite to make my mother happy."

I'm still not sure.

"Wow. Tell me how you really feel," Skylar says from behind me.

I jump from my seated spot, turning to face her.

Beth stands, too, and then shrugs. "Karma," she says and walks off.

"I'll come with you." Skylar turns, ready to follow Beth.

"Please wait," I say reaching for her, pulling my arm back when she stops.

"So you can insult me again?"

"I …" Beth is long gone now, and it's just me and Skylar. I don't even know where to begin. "I was a jerk." Yeah, that's sounds pretty good.

Skylar props her hip against the couch. "Go on."

"All right, so I only asked you if you needed a ride a today because my mother wants more than anything for us to get along. I have no idea why, since you—"

"Did nothing wrong," she cuts in.

"Since you popped into our lives," I say instead of what I was going to say. Clearly I'm predictable, even to her.

"I don't know why she feels this way, but she is my

mother and I should give it a shot. We don't exactly get along. I'll be the first to admit it. But the least we could do is put on a front for her."

"So only be kind to each other when she's around?"

"Yes."

Her lips pucker out as she stares at something behind me.

"Yeah, I don't think that's going to work for me."

"Why not?"

"Because now we are going to be at the store together and working at the bar together. I think we need to give this whole civil thing a real chance."

"And what, be friends?"

"Maybe not right off the bat, but you don't even know me."

"I—"

"—know what you want to think of me. You think I'm a criminal with no goals in life other than making your life miserable, and I think you're an uptight jerk who needs to get a grip on his life and learn that not everyone is out to get him."

"You don't even know me." Not really much of an argument, but I am none of those things she said.

"Finally, something we agree on." Her brow rises and a smug smile appears. "So what do you say, call a truce?"

"That was your lead up?" I laugh. "Tell me I basically suck and then ask me to be friends?"

"Well, you want to please your mom, and I want to keep a job long enough to get my own place. I don't want to be above that bookstore any longer than you want me there. The sooner we get along, the sooner the store is back open and I have my own place. Deal?"

"Now, that sounds like a great plan. I'll see you in the morning."

My hand swallows up her soft and fragile one as we shake on it. I'm not really sure what I just got myself into, but I'm pretty sure the fact I'm already looking forward to seeing her again isn't a good sign.

CHAPTER TEN

Skylar

I can't be attracted to Luke. No way. He's the jerk I, unfortunately by taking this job, will have to see him twice as much as I did before. I thought calling a truce last night was the right thing to do, but now I'm not so sure. I hardly slept last night thinking about how I was going to see him this morning and how it might actually be nice being around him. My heart starts racing every time I think he's about to walk in the door.

I can't be attracted to Luke. I mean, I can—I am—but I don't want to be.

I take the broom I was using earlier and try to sweep up the area behind the counter where the cash register sits. I cleared this area first because we need the counter space and being able to move around it makes hauling books from spot to spot easier. Plus, Luke keeps talking about how he is going to do it, but he never does.

Oh my gosh. I'm already doing things for him. This isn't good.

"Skylar!" Luke yells, stepping through the door at full speed. He halts when he sees me right in front of him. "Oh, sorry, I thought you would still be upstairs. You're usually still getting ready at this time."

Yes, I'm aware I'm not being normal right now.

"Thought I would get a head start." The words come out fast.

"Okay, well." He scratches behind his neck as he turns around. "Before we can do this whole we-work-here-and-work-there thing, we need to set some sort of boundaries."

"You have got to be kidding me. All because I started working at the bar? I have to make money, Luke—what else can I do?"

He sighs, avoiding looking right at me. I look away, too, because the more I stand here, the sexier he is and the more annoyed I get. He is the most frustrating person I know. *How am I attracted to him?*

"What's this?" he asks.

"What's what?" I force myself to gaze in his direction. He holds up my list—that I so stupidly set on the counter, in plain sight after I added a few things to it—and what was my shattered heart leaps into my throat as I refrain myself from lunging at him. He's the last person I want to see that list.

His eyes widen, and I can't take it anymore. I reach for the paper, but he moves quickly, keeping it out of my reach.

"You've never been skinny dipping?"

"Give that to me."

"Have you really never driven a car either?"

"Luke."

"Get a job—we can cross that one off. Get me a pen."

I want to stomp my foot and throw some sort of tantrum from the embarrassment right now, but Luke isn't even looking at me. His eyes scan the list like he's into it.

"How late do you consider sleeping in?"

He asks in such a serious tone that … no, he can't possibly think he's going to help me. This is my list. Not his. He can make his own if he wants.

"Can I have my list back, please?"

"Yeah, sure, but you only have three things crossed off. There should be more."

He grabs my hand.

"Painting your nails pink is the first thing on this list. How have you not done that yet and, more important, why are they red and not pink?"

I think it's safe to say that I have no idea how to respond right now. This is not the Luke I'm used to interacting with. Not even close. This Luke is … dare I say? … in a good mood.

He returns his gaze to the list, and there's a lump in his throat as he swallows. He shoves the paper at me and says, "I can help you with a few of those."

Oh, now I know what he read. My guess is either the "have a one-night stand" line or the "don't wear panties in public" line.

"Thanks for the offer. But I can handle them *all* on my own." I fold the letter up and stuff it in my pocket.

"I meant, we could get you a cake to eat for breakfast. And while we are at the store, you can buy some Ramen noodles and have those for dinner."

Food. He wants to help me with the food goals. I fidget with my hair and run my hands over my shirt. I start to clear more counter space so he can't see the look in my eyes. He could have at least said he'd help me with the ask-a-guy-for-his-number entry.

"Um, sure."

"Cool, let's head there now. I'll even let you drive."

"No, no, no. That—no" is how I answer, my head shaking and my hands waving like there could be a fly in front of my face.

"It's on your list. Let's cross off three in one trip, Sky."

My chest tightens at the thought. That's the first time he's used the nickname everyone here has for me. *It sounds so much better when he says it.*

"Don't we have work to do here, though?"

He looks around the room, nodding. Then he rubs a hand slowly over his mouth before saying, "One day off won't hurt anything."

"I don't want to die before I have the chance to do all the other items, Luke, and I don't have the money to go to the store right now. Hence, why I needed to find a job."

His entire stance goes still.

"My treat then, since I did ruin that for you. And I bet you'll be just fine driving."

"I don't have a license."

"So?"

"What if I get pulled over?"

"You've been arrested for more."

I roll my eyes. *Yes, I have.*

"Maybe next time."

Luke crosses his arms over his chest. He looks me up and

down. It makes me feel weird. Like I should step back, or maybe I should step closer. Should I look at him or look away? Whatever he's doing, it's confusing me so much I don't even know how to feel about it.

"No," he says so loudly that I jump. Then he takes me by the wrist, grabs my purse, and pulls me behind him out the door. "We're also going to stop by the DMV so you can apply for a real license. Add that to the list."

"Luke, wait, this is too much for one day."

"All right, fine, we can go to the DMV tomorrow."

He's already planning to hang out with me tomorrow?

"Luke, this is all very sweet and fully unexpected, but today is supposed to be day one of getting along. Just showing support over my list is good enough for me. You don't have to go all out to prove to everyone you no longer hate me."

We're in the middle of the bookstore when he stops walking. He turns to face me, never letting his hand drop.

"I don't hate you, Sky. You've just placed obstacles in my life that I don't need. It's hard to get past what you did, but everyone seems to like you, and a part of me wants to believe that you really were in the wrong place at the wrong time. Put yourself in my shoes. If you were walking around the corner that night and saw me standing in the doorway to your destroyed store, what would you think?"

"Well, I'd definitely ask questions."

"But you would assume it's me, wouldn't you?"

I can't look at him now, as much as he is begging me to look him in the eyes. He's right. If the tables were turned, I'd have blamed him, too.

"I would have apologized once there was no evidence, though," I say.

"Even if you didn't know me, you'd just believe the authorities?" he asks.

I let his words sink in. Maybe it was easier for him to accept I did it than to know he might never know who it really was.

"I would have made an effort." This time, I have no choice but to meet his eyes. Deep blue stares back at me, and if I see right, there's an apology in them.

"Is it too late for me to start?"

My lips clearly have no self-control as they break into a smile, and I nod.

"Let's just hope I don't kill us first," I answer, plucking his keys out of his fingers and passing him to the door.

If he wants to offer to help with more on my list, I just might let him. Go big or go home, right? And I'm definitely not going home.

Luke

"Brake! Hit the brake!"

"I don't—"

"Keep your hands on the wheel!"

"I can't do this!" she yells back, ending our shouting match as my car jerks to a stop in the middle of the road. I twist to look behind us. No cars. *Whew.* I rub my hands over my face before facing her again.

"Okay, so this is going to take some practice."

Sky is staring straight ahead, her small fingers twisted in a death grip around the top of the steering wheel. I'd told her ten and two when she got in, and I don't think she has left that spot except for switching gears.

"Hey, whoa, why are you crying?" I ask, my pulse racing more now at the sight of her than it was a minute ago when we were still on the road.

"I can't drive. I almost just killed us. I couldn't even buy my own piece of cake. I'm lucky those noodle things were only ten cents apiece." She takes a deep breath, releasing her hands and wiping under eyes. "Can you please just drive us back?"

I unclip my belt and get out. She doesn't move as I walk around the hood of the car. When I get to her door, she slowly opens it. She steps out with her head down. I move in front of her and tilt her chin up when she stops.

"I'm sorry I yelled. That was 100 percent bad-teacher behavior on my side."

"It's not your fault; I should have learned this so, *so* long ago, but my parents didn't think it was something I ever needed to know. I believed them, too, until one day … I just didn't anymore."

She makes her way to the passenger's side, and after we both get in, I slowly head back to the bookstore. If I've learned anything from my mom and sisters, it's that when a lady is upset, you give her space and silence until she is ready to talk. So that's what I do now. She tucks her knees to her chest and looks out the window.

I always thought she was attractive. And I thought by her petite frame that she took great care of herself, but after what she said earlier about needing a job to buy food, I've really looked at her. She's too skinny. She reached up for a box of crackers and her hipbone peeked out from her shirt. While walking next to her, I stole a few glances: her wrist bone sticks out. I guarantee my pinky and thumb could wrap around her bicep and touch. She needs to eat, and I'm the jerk who kept her from that. It took a lot not to buy her the whole damn store.

But it makes no sense. If she came from money, why not keep enough to buy food? I thought that Alex and Beth had brought her some when she moved into the apartment. Is she not eating it?

I park in front of the store. We meet at the trunk to grab the bags. I follow her inside, still in silence. After we set the bags on the counter, I stand in her kitchen. I feel like I need to be here until I witness her eating something. But the best choice I can make is to probably give her some privacy.

"Should we eat the cake or the noodles first?" she asks just as I'm about to head for the door.

"The cake," I say all too quickly, digging it from the bag and handing her a fork from the drawer. I lucked out with the fact she left the silverware in the drawer where it's always been. I also picked the cake because we don't have to cook it, so she can eat now.

She sits down at the table, a giant smile on her face. She picked red velvet cake, and I didn't argue. I start to put the rest of the food away, waiting impatiently for her to take the first bite. When she does, her eyes light up just before she goes in for a second and a third bite. After the fourth bite, she looks up. Her mouth is full of cake.

"Oh, did you want some?" She laughs, covering her mouth.

I laugh, too, because this is the happiest I've ever seen her.

Pulling the list from her pocket, Sky unfolds it over the table. She clicks the top of a pen and draws a line across it.

"It's not even ten yet—this definitely counts as breakfast."

"It definitely counts," I reply. "You can make these noodles for lunch, and then you can cross off that and learning to drive a car."

"Except I didn't actually learn to drive a car, and how do I make them?"

"You did learn, you just suck at it, and I'll be here to show you how to make them."

"Wow," she says.

"What?"

"You really can be as kind as everyone said. Either that, or your mother has bribed you with something good this time." She raises her brow as she grins, licking the last of the frosting off her fork.

I deserved that.

"No, she didn't. This is me just being me. Mom would actually be very impressed. She thinks it's far too long since her son has been around."

And I've never felt more like myself.

"Why would she think that?"

"She just … she worries, a lot" is how I answer because going into my whole life story isn't something I need to share or probably anything Sky even cares about.

"Well, from a kid who grew up with parents who didn't care at all, you're lucky to have a mom like her. She's never actually told me so, but from how I've seen her look you at you. I don't think you could ever disappoint her. What you're doing to keep your family store up and going is amazing."

"Yeah, it was my dad's favorite place to be, and I'd be lying if I said I didn't love the place myself."

"I hate to be stereotypical, but it still amazes me that a good looking guy like you who clearly likes to work out and play sports is into books."

"Well, in that case, there are a lot of things about me that might surprise you."

"Like what?" she asks.

"I guess you'll have to find out."

"Ha."

"So, tell me about you." I take the seat across from her. "How did you end up in Wind Valley, Wyoming, and more importantly, how did you end up homeless?"

She picks up the fork, staring at it a moment, and then puts it down.

"That's a story for another day, but the short version is, I wanted to be the exact opposite of what I was."

"And are you?"

She pauses. "I guess you'll have to find out."

My cell buzzes in my pocket while I try to think of something smart to say.

Mom: How is the store coming along today?

Sky rises from the table, smiling at me as she does so, then she winks and I have to look away. We went from our act of friendship to flirting in her apartment in a matter of hours.

• • •

Luke: It's looking better than before.

And, man, is it ever.

CHAPTER ELEVEN

Skylar

The last couple of weeks have been some of the best I can ever remember, minus the day when some guys showed up with a new window and then shattered it as they were attempting to put it in. I luckily spent most of that day at the pet shelter. Oh, and then the one day Luke had to reschedule again with the inspector. That phone call was painful to listen to. From what I gathered, the inspector isn't in any rush to make it to the store on Luke's schedule. I avoided him for a few hours after he hung up.

But yeah, other than that, it's been great.

Oddly enough, most of it is thanks to Luke. Because of him I can officially drive a car—without slamming on the brakes, I might add. We haven't fought once except over my fully stocked fridge—I fought this one, but he won—and that really wasn't even a fight. We've actually been doing more flirting than anything else. My nails are hot pink, I've had cake for breakfast twice, we ate cookie dough ice cream right out of the carton, and Ramen noodles are my new favorite meal. Completely horrible for you, but I love them. One week with Luke and I've crossed four things off my list. We should have done this friends thing a long time ago.

I shift his car into park and switch off the engine.

"You're almost a pro," he says, getting out.

"I've had a pretty good teacher."

"I would have to say I agree with you." He flashes a grin my way. It's a grin I've noticed a lot in the last few days.

The alarm chirps once I've locked it, and I toss him his keys over the top of the car.

"Is this real?" Conner yells from the back door of the BA. I've only been back once for a walk-through. Tonight is my first official night of training. I'm freaking out about the whole bartending thing, but with Luke and Beth here, I'll be okay.

Luke doesn't answer Conner as we head his way. I don't either because it's clear he's waiting for a response from Luke. Conner gestures to the car.

"You've never let anyone, and I mean *anyone*, not even your mom, drive that car, and here you pull up with Sky in the driver's seat."

I stop—*really, not even his mom?*—but Luke keeps walking, nudging me to continue as well. His touch practically burns through my shirt. I get this feeling every time we come in contact. Always unintentionally, of course.

"I was just teaching her to drive. It's not a big deal."

"What? And she's a beginner." Conner slaps his hands together, chuckling as he follows us inside.

Luke goes straight for the computer, tapping in his

employee number to clock in, and I do the same after he teaches me what to do.

I start to follow Luke around, filling sinks with cleaning water, checking the soda pumps to make sure they don't need to be changed, and double-checking that certain areas of the bar are stocked. About thirty minutes go by before other employees begin to arrive for their shift. Beth is one of them, and the only other girl working is Abby. I don't know much about her other than she works at the gym and she went to school with Beth, Sara, Luke, and Kelsey. I've heard people talk about her, and I don't think it's a bad thing that I haven't gotten to know her. The fact she keeps glaring at me is a bit annoying though.

Conner gathers the group to go over some of the evening's duties, along with introducing me to everyone. It's like the AA meetings you see on TV: everyone super enthusiastically says "Hi, Sky" back to me, and I cringe because they laugh at the fact it rhymes.

"You seriously don't know how to make any kind of drink?" Luke asks when a customer orders the first beer.

I may have told Sara I knew the basics to get the job.

"I do, just not anything with alcohol in it," I say. That part is true.

"You've never even mixed a drink at a party before?"

I blink, not knowing what to say. The types of parties he's been too are probably not the same as the ones I went to. In fact, I hardly even drank because my father and my ex-fiancé always got drunk to the point they passed out, and Mom always ended up telling people Dad had to leave early for a meeting. He never drank at home though, only at parties. And even when I moved in with Mack, there was always a butler there to make my father's drinks. The point is, I've never had to make a drink for anyone.

My eyes find Luke's again, and I shrug.

He shakes his head, a grin taking over. He fills another glass with beer and then sets all the glasses he just filled onto a tray with a ticket.

"Okay, so how about tonight we start with something easy? I'll show you how to make a couple of drinks, ones that only involve a few ingredients, and when it gets busy you can be in charge of pouring beers."

"I can manage that."

"Have you ever drawn beer from a tap before?"

My nose wrinkles as I give him a full-toothed smile.

He chuckles. "Okay, come here. The names are pretty easy. We keep only ten different beers on tap. The names are here." He points to the top of each spout. "If the customer wants a bottle, you can find those down here." He points to the lower half of the counter, which is a fridge. In fact, the entire lower half of the bar isn't storage but half refrigerators. All filled to the clear glass doors with bottles of beer.

"You just grab the one they want, pop the top, and hand it to them." He twists the top off and hands it to a guy pulling up a seat at the bar. I hope everyone in the town is a bottle drinker because there is no way I can mess that up.

I step back to move out of Luke's way as the printer starts to go off. He steps forward at the same time. His chest brushes my backside, and I straighten as his hands grip my arms to steady me. I expect him to keep moving, but he doesn't. Instead he pauses, too, and I can feel the pressure of his chest against my back as he inhales.

"Sorry, it can get a little tight back here sometimes."

"It's fine," I say and turn to face him. His eyes flash between mine and my lips, and he isn't doing anything to create space between us. I really like this job, but it's safe to assume I'm not going to be good at it.

Luke

This girl is driving me absolutely crazy.

She couldn't pour a beer if her life depended on it. She's broken at least three glasses and has spilled, at minimum, four bottles. She's a wreck, and our tips are low tonight. I should be angry. I need that money. My family needs it, and this is going to force me to pick up another shift here when I'm not training. I've already put myself behind at the store by spending more time bullshitting with her during the day than fixing something, anything. Then again, I'm still waiting on the inspector, so I have some time to solve that problem. Sooner or later, she'll be here at the BA when I'm not and then I'll get things done at the store.

Shattering glass captures my attention. I glance over my shoulder and spot Sky standing there with her eyes wide and a hand over her mouth. I wiggle four fingers in the air, and her head drops back so she looking at the ceiling as her arms fall to her sides.

As much of a hot mess Sky is as a bartender, she is too cute for her own good, and I know she's trying her best. That's what I'm pissed about. Two weeks and I'm more into her than any other girl I've ever met. She has all these ideas for the bookstore, which are great and I want to do them, but I also want to sell the store. Then again, she is so excited about what I can do with the place that I feel like I could be successful and maybe I shouldn't sell.

I read somewhere that sometimes when a person develops strong feelings of any kind—in my case, anger and distrust—the power they bring out can turn into the opposite emotion. As if the first set of feelings are a mask for the real ones. I thought it was complete bullshit until this moment. Sky is last person on this earth I should trust or could ever imagine myself being with, yet I can't seem to get my mind and body to stop reacting to her. If I'm honest, I'm not completely sure I want to.

"You two seem to be getting along pretty well." Beth slides the round tray my way as I retrieve more tickets from the printer. "Is this more to do with what your mother wants, or are you two actually getting along?"

I don't answer her right away because the tone in her voice hints she has a hunch it's the latter, plus some. And by not answering, I can hide the smile that my lips are straining to hold back. I like Sky, but I don't think everyone needs to know about it.

"Guys and girls can be just friends," I tell her, turning to grab a bottle of vodka. "Look at us."

I twist back around. Beth is looking back and forth between me and Sky. Sky has no idea anyone is watching her, and a light chuckle comes from inside me at her furrowed brow as she holds the bottle and the shot glass next to each other. Trying to figure how to put it on the bottle, no doubt.

"Well, I sure hope you puked on her, too, and she put you in the friend zone because that look on your face doesn't say just friends, Luke. And if she did friend zone you, vomit or not, I'd say you're lying to me or yourself."

"Beth, can't two people just … I don't know, be, without having to be either just friends or more than friends?"

The shocked look on her face matches how I feel about what I just said. I hadn't planned to say that. I know I've been curious if there could be a "me and Sky"—and there could be—but Conner said she is from money, and that throws me off. I'm struggling to support my family and here she is, not caring that someone worked hard for her to have the life she left. It doesn't seem right.

"You let her drive your car. I don't think you have much to think about," Conner adds as he walks by.

"What are we *thinking* about?" Sky asks, walking up behind Conner. Beth slides off her chair, taking the drinks I just made, and heads in the direction of her tables.

Cheerful eyes smile at me as Sky waits for me to say something. I'm still a little stuck on how she said *we*.

"About whether or not I should teach you how to bake a cake after work. It is on your list and all," I say quickly. I just invited myself to her place. Usually, it's us hanging out at the store. Only that first day were we alone in her apartment. This could be a bad idea.

"Luke, I would love to learn how to bake a cake. But, honestly, you've done so much for me that I think I need to give you a break from being forced to spend all your free time with me."

Beth is walking back by this time and mouths "free time" with raised brows at me. I glance away quickly. I'm aware I've spent more time lately with Sky than anyone else in the last year outside of work.

"I'm not being forced," I say to Sky.

She smiles up at me. "Rain check?"

"Of course." I smile back, although I can feel it's forced. That was kind of like me asking her out, wasn't it? *Out* out, to hang out—same thing, isn't it? But she said no. Sky gives me a shoulder bump as she passes, and thank god she can't see how big my eyes must be right now. She said no and she shoulder bumped me. Officially friend zone behavior. I've clearly been reading all her signs wrong.

I glance over my shoulder where she is now behind the counter, talking to a man ordering drinks. She smiles at me, winks, and turns back to the guy in front of her.

Yeah, I should probably be the one who takes male customers' orders from here on out.

CHAPTER TWELVE

Skylar

"So, let me get this right. You came from Washington to Wyoming because you had too much money?"

Well, when she puts it like that, it makes me sound like a spoiled brat. I always find it awkward to explain without having to give too much personal detail. Growing up, my father was strict, and he made sure we knew all he did for us. Younger me was always thankful, but the older I got, the more I resented my father's bragging. When Mack and I first got engaged I had hoped he would be nothing like my father, but I was wrong. Mack's mindset about money grew worse by the day. He always made sure I knew how much he *sacrificed* for me to benefit from that deal. As if I needed reminding that he made the money. Because of that, he acted like he owned me. I had to wear this, look like that, or say only certain things. I despise how money can transform a person's view on other people and the world around them. That view on life isn't something I support. I never knew how other people lived, but I knew I wanted to find out.

"Mainly because I had no idea who I was, and I sort of still don't. I mean, I'm working on that" is how I sum it up.

I like the way my life has been lately. Getting along with Luke makes me feel like I'm starting to belong here. The people I've made friends with have given me all the confidence I need to know I'm fully capable of taking care of myself, and Luke must have just been the last piece I needed for things to click.

"How could someone not know who they are? I'm going to need an example." With her wine glass to her lips, Beth finishes off her glass of moscato.

"Hmm. Oh, I have this list."

I stand to grab the list off the counter and some of the wine in my glass sloshes over the side. I stop, gulp back the rest as if I were chugging a beer before grabbing the list and another bottle from the fridge.

After Luke mentioned coming to my place a couple nights ago, some trigger went off through my entire body. It took everything I had to say rain check. That was the moment I learned how much I look forward to being around Luke, and that's why Beth agreed to come over and hang out with me tonight. To distract me. Only she doesn't know, and that's okay, because it's working, for the most part.

She brought over some food and three bottles of wine, said I needed to stock up till I was making more money in tips. If I'm going through two bottles a night, I better start practicing how to make drinks even if I'm not at the bar.

I plop back down on the bed and shove the list at her. I

refill her glass as she reads and then I fill my own. I lean toward the nightstand to set the bottle down when it occurs to me I've never drunk alcohol from the bottle. I don't even need to add it to the list to know it's something I want to do. Bottle to my lips, I take two huge gulps—*shoot, that burns*—and then cough, wine spilling from the corners of my mouth.

Beth's eyes are huge.

"Soooo, are we crossing off 'get wasted' on the list?"

Oh, it feels so good to laugh and not be in trouble for rebelling. Technically, it isn't rebelling anymore if I can do what I want.

"I don't think I'm drunk."

"That's what a drunk person would say."

"No, when I wrote that, I meant it as I-go-to-an-actual-bar-and-someone-has-to-carry-me- out style drunk."

"So, you want to get black-out plastered, do you?"

"Exactly."

"If I had a list like this, I'd want to do that, too." She claps her hands together. "Okay, we are going to the bar to cross one or two of these things off your list tonight."

"What, no, we can't do that." Luke is helping with that list. If I have Beth help me, he'll think I replaced him. And I want him to help me with some other things on that list.

Maybe I am drunk.

"Who says we can't?"

"Well, I have to be here," I say.

"Where?"

"At the bookstore."

"Why?"

"Umm," Yeah … I don't have an answer for that.

"Because …" I try again. *What if Luke were to show up and I wasn't here?*

"I thought you were trying to figure what kind of person you are. Are you the kind to follow the rules or break them?"

Oh, I'm breaking rules now? Tempting.

"Hmmm, we won't go to jail, will we?"

"No, girl, once is enough for you, I think."

She is off the bed before I can shove her, and I lose my balance, steadying myself with the nightstand.

"Maybe we should wait till another night," she suggests.

"No, I totes want to be someone who goes to a bar tonight." Tipsy Sky must be easily convinced.

"Totes?"

"Yeah, it sounded weird in my head, too. Guess I'm not the kind of girl to shorten up words. Totally sounds way better," I say, quickly followed by, "Which bar are we going to?"

Beth tosses a blue and green tunic blouse that is cut off at the shoulders at me. I've already got on brown leggings.

"Oh, toss me my flats," I say.

"I think you should wear these shoes." She holds up a pair of wedges. "And we're going to the BA."

I burst into laughter, and she clearly missed the joke.

"I can't even keep my balance sitting on this bed and you want me to wear a heel?"

"Touché," she says and reluctantly hands me the shoes I asked for.

Beth has on ripped jeans and a t-shirt. She rocks this outfit all the time. Her beautiful red hair I envy so much—I always wanted to be Ariel, she was my favorite princess—is loosely braided to the side.

I surprise myself when I make it down the stairs and through the store with no error in my steps. Beth's Nitro chirps and I step toward it.

"Where are you going?" she asks.

"To get in."

"Um, no, I've drunk two glasses of wine already, and you're giving off the three-bottle vibe right now. It's a couple of blocks—we can walk. I was only locking my car."

I just laugh.

That must be my thing when I laugh. Oh no, I mean when I drink. Here I go, laughing again.

Beth plays on her phone for the entire walk. When she pushes open the door for me, I spot my list in her hand and pluck it from her fingers.

"Why did you bring this?"

"Because we're going to cross off a few things."

"Like what? I don't have show the whole world on my list." I'm all about trying new things, but I'm curious as to which she thinks I should do. Especially here.

"Hmmm." She glances around. Her body straightens as she stands tall and smiles. I follow her gaze to a man looking up from the jukebox. He's cute, in that light haired, boy-next-door sort of way.

"Okay, kiss a stranger."

"What?" I laugh. "I can't do that."

"Yeah, I pick that guy."

Boy-Next-Door is now walking our way. He's smiling, and now I'm smiling, and then he's right here in front of me. Before I can think any more on it, I push up on my toes, rest my hands on his chest, and press my lips against his. He stumbles, steadying me, all while kissing me back.

A tongue touches my lip; I pull back. That counts. That totally counts.

"Hey, Tyler," Beth says. "This is my friend, Sky. Sky, this is Tyler."

"You know him?" I practically gasp. "That doesn't count as a stranger."

"I know him, you do not."

Huh.

"Hi," he says, grinning at me.

"Hi," I say. *Is the heat on?* Surely, it's on high.

I wrote *stranger* on the list so I wouldn't have to chat with him after. Oh well, I'm still counting it.

"Are you new here?" he asks.

"Beth," a loud voice booms, and I jump. Luke is standing behind the bar with his arms crossed. He looks furious. My heartbeat speeds up. Furious Luke is sexy. Which is weird, because when he was always mad at me, I never considered him to be hot. Well, not this hot. Maybe it's because this time he said Beth's name, and maybe that means he's mad at her and not me.

I catch a small movement of his hand. Does he want me to go over there?

"I'll catch up with you two in a minute," she says, heading for the bar. Luke is shaking his head now.

"Skylar," Luke says my name this time, not as intensely as he said Beth's though, and waves me over.

"So ..."

"I'll catch up with you later, too, then." Tyler looks bummed but doesn't waste time heading back to the area where he was standing when we came in. Me, however, I just keeping standing in the same spot.

What does Luke want? We've spent a lot of time together lately. I figured he'd be ready for a night without me around.

With small steps, I start moving toward the bar. Beth pats the seat next to her.

"What's wrong with him?" I whisper. Luke is standing at the other end. Perhaps I didn't ask softly enough, because he glances to look at me.

"No clue, but I ordered us shots."

"My first shot!"

"Oh boy, we are in for a night."

I start nodding. I look toward Tyler, who is smiling at me, but Luke has no exact, distinguishable expression on his face. I swallow and the room grows even warmer than before.

Yep, we sure are.

Luke

Kissing.

They were fucking kissing. That's not good at all.

"You all right?" Conner asks. "You're not going to break that glass, are you?"

I loosen my grip on the cup in my hand. "Yeah, I'm fine, just a lot on my mind."

"You and Tyler fighting or something?"

"No, why?"

"Oh, maybe because you keep looking at him like you're about to kill him."

Shit, am I?

I sigh and focus on mixing drinks.

"Does this have anything to do with Sky?"

"Why does everything keep coming back to her?"

"Probably because the two of you have been spending a lot of time together. First you hated her and couldn't stand to be around her. Now, if I can find one of you, the other is nearby."

"That has nothing to do with me wanting to be around her. It has to do with the fact that I was already barely meeting ends meet between the store and being here to pay for the store, helping my mother out, and paying my own bills before the place was vandalized. We are working together to get the place up and running is all."

I know it's a lie even as I say it.

"And how far along is the store coming?" he asks in an overly curious tone. I choose not to answer his question. He knows Sky and I haven't made much progress since we started getting along. Mainly because I should be livid the inspector booked me out again. At this rate, he'll never show up. But every day that passes and he isn't there is one more day I get to spend time with Sky. And that, I don't mind it at all.

"Luke, you don't have to hide the fact that you're spending more time with a girl than on the store. In fact, I'm happy you're putting yourself first for once."

"Luke! Where are our shots?" Beth hollers. I rush to mix them—I should have been doing that this whole time—thankful that I have something focus on instead of replying to Conner. What would I have said to him?

You've got it all wrong, because my family and the store come first. Nope, I can't say that.

He's right.

Shots in hand, I head down to stand in front of Beth and Sky.

"What brings you two out?" I ask, my attempt at focusing my mind on anything else.

"Sky has this bucket list, and we are out tonight trying to fulfill a few of the things she wrote down."

Oh, thank god. She was probably only kissing Tyler to cross something off her list. I have to hold back my smile. It wasn't even a real kiss.

"Make me another drink, please," Sky cuts in and throws back her shot. Her eyes bug out, and her hand shoots to cover mouth as her foot taps against the ground. "That was awful. What was that?"

Sky reaches for the soda gun. I swat her hand away and pour her a glass of Coke before sliding it to her. She gulps it down.

"So much better," she says, but it doesn't come out as clearly as she meant for it to. A new song comes over the speakers, a song I'm not familiar with, but Sky apparently loves it. She stands quickly.

"Beth, let's dance." She cheers with excitement.

"No, I'm good," Beth answers, turning to face me as Sky heads for the dance floor alone.

"She may have had more alcohol than normal tonight." Beth laughs.

"I can see that."

I never let Sky out of my view during the last hour of my shift. Occasionally, she comes back to the bar for a drink before returning to the dance floor. She's the only one there now, so when she falls and doesn't push herself up, I know it's time to get her home.

I close out the last few drinks I need to make, and then I meet Beth out front. She and Sky are sitting on the bench.

Well, Beth is sitting, Sky is leaning over, resting her head on Beth's shoulder.

Her eyes are closed and her arms are crossed in front of her. A loose hair falls in front of her face, and she swipes it away. Beth's brow peaks before her gaze moves to Sky, who seems to be attempting to get as close to Beth as she can. I shake my head.

"I hate to break that lust filled gaze in your eyes," Beth begins, "but I have to be somewhere. I'll come back for my car later."

"Where could you have to be at this time?" I ask, hooking my arm around Sky to prop her up to her feet. She moves with me, not letting her weight hang on me like others who have had too much to drink would do.

Beth lets go of Sky's hand when she's aware I've got a good hold on her.

"That's none of your business," she says with a smile. "Just please make sure she gets to bed for me. I trust you, Luke. I don't know what's going on with you two, but make sure she is safe."

"Of all people, you know I will, Beth."

"I know." Her smile is gone when she turns to head in the other direction.

Sky looks so peaceful and innocent. With a shrug, I lift her a little higher and start walking. She walks with me, her steps slow and dragging against the cement sidewalk. After the second stumble because she can't seem to pick her feet up all the way, I swing her legs up and carry her.

She slides one hand around the back of my neck to lock with the other and then buries her face into my shirt.

"I hate that you always smell so good, Luke."

I swallow, affected by her saying my name or the way she moans when she finishes smelling my shirt. I'm not going to say anything because she's drunk and she doesn't know what she's saying.

"I didn't do it, Luke. I didn't break in."

I keep on with my silence. After a minute or two, I hear her sniffle. I feel the moment my shirt absorbs her tears.

"I really wish I could find the people who did it. I'd love to see them pay."

I slow my steps … every word she's saying is clear. She hasn't slurred a single word since she was sitting at the bar.

"I wish I were a detective"—her slurred words are back—"because then I would find them and show you it wasn't me."

"Sky."

"Someone has to find them, Luke, otherwise this will never be good."

"Things are good now."

"No, they aren't."

"We get along just fine; how is that not good?"

"Because I don't want to be just your friend anymore. I've never got to choose who I wanted to date, and now that I can, he thinks I'm a criminal."

I stop. We're at the corner of the bookstore. She must notice that we aren't moving anymore because she wiggles until I put her down. Her walk isn't anything close to a straight line, so I follow her. She never continues with what she said. I don't ask her about it either, because I know how I feel and I know she flirts, but I guess I didn't think she wanted anything to come of it. We don't know that much about each other still. But at some point in this last week, I've come to terms that she probably wasn't the one who broke in.

I unlock the door and wait until Sky disappears inside before I lock it behind her.

Do I move past all this and ask her out for real, make time for a girlfriend, or tell her that being friends is the best thing for me until I can get my family back on track?

CHAPTER THIRTEEN

Skylar

It's almost been a week since I successfully crossed getting wasted off my list and made an ass out of myself in front of Luke. I remember what I said, and I know he does, too. He just hasn't said anything about it, nor has he acted any differently.

He doesn't even seem to mind that I spend a few hours every morning at the animal shelter instead of at the store. It's probably for the best. Forget I even said anything.

"Listen up!" Logan and Sara both step out of the office. Luke and I are at one end, and Conner, Beth, and Abby are all at the other end of the bar. Everyone makes their way to center as Logan waves a piece of paper in the air and Sara follows behind him with wide grin.

"Tonight will more than likely get busy after the college basketball game. Sara and I have decided to make this night fun for everyone. If it goes well, we may make it a weekend tradition."

"Work's already a blast, Logan." Beth's sarcastic humor gains a laugh from everyone.

"Ha ha, funny girl. You'll actually mean those words when tonight is over. So here are the rules."

"Rules for what?" Luke asks. His curious tone matches spot on with the one inside my head.

"A game," Sara answers him.

Luke crosses his arms as his hip leans against the counter. I'm more focused now on how his shoulder is resting against me than whatever Logan is about to say.

"It's a bit random, but here." He begins to hand out a sheet of paper to each of us. A new customer steps up to the bar, so Logan pauses to allow Luke to serve them before he continues.

"The list of drinks on the paper in front of you is the game. Be the first to sell each of those drinks in any order and you win. Now, let's select your teams."

"Men versus women," Beth says quickly.

"No, that makes three against two. Not fair," Conner says.

"Afraid you're going to lose?" Abby pipes up next to him with a look that could catch fire.

"No, Conner and I could outsell all you easily," Luke chimes in.

"Twice," Conner adds.

"Doubt it," Beth replies to them both. "New rule, the first group to make it through this list twice wins."

"Whoa, whoa," Logan says, but it's clear they aren't listening to him.

"And if neither team makes it through twice?" Conner's hands find his hips as he waits for Beth's answer.

"It's a draw and we try again another night."

"Deal."

"Deal."

Abby rolls her eyes as Conner, Luke, and Beth all shake on the rules. "I'm not playing this stupid game," she says, walking off.

Beth shrugs. "Sky, you're in, right?"

"Yeah, sure, but I'm still not very good."

"We just have to sell them and ring them in first."

I nod, and as I'm about to turn, I pause. Logan and Sara are standing on the other side of the bar, watching us all with blank expressions.

"What?" Luke asks.

"That was not the game we planned," Logan says.

"Not even close," Sara says. "It's way better, but I'm curious, what do you guys think you're winning?"

Everyone trades a glance.

"A free shift off?" Conner suggests.

"I was thinking more like dinner on us one night." Logan laughs.

"Works for me," I say, finally adding my voice to this conversation.

"And the satisfaction of proving these two wrong," Beth says.

"Ditto," Luke says.

"If we don't get this last drink, we're going to lose. All my badass talk will have been for nothing," Beth says close to the end of the night.

"I know I'm trying. If I hadn't broken those glasses, I

wouldn't have been busy cleaning up my mess and I could have been helping customers." I sigh. Beth should have known it would be a challenge with me on her team.

"You're absolutely right. Want to make it up to me?"

"How?" My head tilts as I narrow my eyes at her. The way she said that, I'd say she already has an idea.

"Distract Luke."

I laugh. "Luke and I haven't exactly been … I don't know. I just don't think I can do it."

"Maybe, maybe not, but you better figure it out quick, because that guy who just walked in? He's our ticket to winning. Now get on it!" She smacks my butt as I head in the direction of our newest customer, who is headed right for Luke. With a bit of a gallop-skip thing, I'm by Luke's side, smiling at the gentleman.

"Hi, what can I get you?" I ask.

"Let me think for just a moment. I can't decide if it's a vodka night or a whiskey night."

"I'd say it's a vodka night, and I have just the right drink for you," Luke says before I can reply. The man nods. Crap, how am I going to distract him before he can ring in that drink and make it? It has to be something totally off the wall. Something good. Something to give me his full focus.

"Luke," I say, touching his forearm and gently tugging for him to face me. The moment he does, I press myself to the tips of my toes. His eyes widen when he realizes what I'm about to do, and the funny thing is, he closes the gap between us, sealing my lips to his. He tastes like spearmint and smells like spices. I graze his biceps, admiring the softness of his skin as an arm snakes around my back and he kisses me deeper, leaning me back just slightly in the process. Before I know it, his tongue has crossed over my lips and my hand is tugging at his hair. What started as a gentle, innocent kiss has quickly turned desperate. It's when I moan into his mouth and my back bumps the counter that I hear the whistling.

I touch my lips the moment they are parted from Luke's. I've never seen this look in his eyes before. Are they are telling me he wants to do that again?

"There you are, sir, vodka soda." Beth's cheery voice is right next to my ear.

We make side eye contact. Her eyes are full of happy concern; I hope mine are giving nothing away.

Luke slowly removes the arm wrapped around me as Conner comes storming our way.

"Beth, you cheated! Sending her in to kiss him was a low move," he says.

"Hey," Beth holds her hands up, "I told her to distract him. Kissing him was all her idea."

I can feel both my cheeks heating and Luke's gaze on me. The grin I find when my eyes meet his is not what I'm expecting. The chuckle that follows leaves my heart ready to explode.

"Can I walk you home tonight?" he asks.

"What?"

That's not what I was thinking he would say. Be mad, sure, but smiling and offering to walk me home?

"Can I walk you home? To the bookstore."

"Umm."

"Yes!" Beth screams. "I'll even close for you, Luke, so you two can head out in about an hour."

Luke nods, resuming his bartender duties, and an hour later we are under the stars and headed down the block.

. . .

Luke

Skylar hasn't spoken since we left the BA. It's fine with me because I asked her on impulse, and although I'm not regretting it, I'm still at a loss for words. When she kissed me, it was like something inside me woke up. I know I was smiling like a damn idiot the rest of our shift, but I couldn't help it. My lips actually freaking felt like they were tingling from her kiss. How is that possible? I touch them now, the feeling coming back to me. How pissed would she be if we did it again?

"I'm sorry," she says, gaining my attention.

"For what?" I ask, even though I know.

"Luke ..."

The way she says my name is growing on me.

"Well, you're not forgiven," I say. I don't want her to regret it.

"Seriously? Why not?"

"Because I'm glad you did it, and I don't care if I sound like a girl when I say that."

Her smile is wide and beautiful.

Every moment with her, I like her more and more. When she wanted to go to the pet shelter for a few hours every day, I agreed because it would give me time to clear my head and actually get some things done at the store, but all it did was make me realize I miss her. And now—now I want to make out with her in full high school, we-could-get-caught-by-my-parents style.

I unlock the door to the bookstore, holding it open for her to enter. When I step in behind her, she pauses.

"What are you doing?" she asks. Her arms brushes against my chest as she turns to face me.

"Walking you to your door."

"Why?"

"Because I can."

"I don't think you should do that," she says in soft whisper.

"Why not?" I take a step toward her.

"It's a bad idea, Luke."

"I think it's a great idea." I reach an arm out, resting my palm flat on the wall next to her head. "The other night you said you didn't want to be just friends."

"Ah, yes, yes, I did."

I lean in.

"Right here is far enough," she says, ducking under my arm. I move fast, wrapping my fingers around her wrist. She twists around, and I lock my lips on hers before she protests anymore. I must have chosen the right time because it doesn't take her even a moment's thought to kiss me back or to run her fingers through my hair as she holds my head in place. She has nothing to worry about—I'm not going anywhere.

It feels like all time has stopped, and when we finally pull away from each other, she's glowing. Sounds lame, I know. But I've never seen the smile that's on her face right now.

I step back because I haven't been with a woman in a few months and my body is already pulling toward her. If I don't leave now—well, I'd love to think about what would happen, but that's exactly why I need to leave.

"I'll see you tomorrow," I say, brushing my fingers against my lips the exact way she's doing now. Is this motion going to happen every time we kiss? Because at this rate, I'll be touching my lips all day, every day.

"Good night, Luke."

Indeed, it is.

Skylar's watching me out of the window, and I keep walking backward, staring right back at her, until I hear the faint click of the lock and she disappears.

I've been dead set against a relationship. I have plenty of responsibilities I should be focusing on, but, tonight from the moment she kissed me, I haven't thought about any of that and it feels fantastic. It feels … like me.

As if on cue, my cell phone buzzes. Brandy's name appears, and as my thumb hovers over the green button, glass breaks somewhere behind me.

Shoving my cell in my front pocket, I take off at a sprint, rounding the corner back to the store.

Sky.

The main window is busted this time, and Sky is standing in the middle of the room holding a rock.

"What the fuck?" I yell.

She gasps and the rock drops.

She couldn't let me have just one night—*one night*—without adding stress back into my life. But this time, I caught her with the rock, her weapon if you want to call it that, to break the glass. She isn't getting away with it this time.

"You can't be serious. Again!" I barge through the door.

"It wasn't me!" she yells back, although it comes out choked up because she's crying and shaking. "I had just slipped on my pajama shorts when I heard the glass. I thought you came back and something happened, but when I came down the stairs, the window was broken and this rock was lying on the floor."

It's not a big rock, and the damage isn't nearly as bad as the first go-around, but right now, I could throw the damn rock through someone else's window because, yeah, I have to order a third fucking window.

"Why are you trying to destroy something so important to me?" My steps are quick as I approach her. "Tell me, Skylar, why do you feel this need to do this shit?"

"I didn't do it."

"Sticking with that same story, are you? Total bullshit, and you know it. I saw you with the rock. You won't get out of it this time."

"What? No. I was upstairs, Luke. I heard the noise and came down here."

"Stop lying to me!"

"I'm not!"

I start to pace. *Fucking shit fuck.* This is fucking ridiculous. How many times can a person say *fuck* till it calms them down? Maybe a few more times. *Fuck. Fuck. Fuck.*

"Luke, I swear to you it wasn't me. Look, I've already changed into my pajamas," she says, holding her arms out, as if this is going to help me see her clothes.

I look her up and down. She couldn't have changed that fast and come back down here. Or she could have planned this: stashed the clothes in a corner and changed once I left, then went outside and threw the rock through the window.

I groan, rubbing my hands over my face. I'm losing my mind.

"Then who is it?" I ask her, defeated.

"I wish I knew. All I know from the first time around was

there were two people, identical in every way I could see: height, clothing, the way they ran. They came out of the store and ran off to the east. That was it."

My head snaps up.

"Identical? Like how tall, do you think?"

She shrugs.

"I was a good distance away; I couldn't give you a for sure answer on that," she says, taking a step toward me. "Luke, I swear, it was not me. This time or the last."

I nod, knowing she's right. But twins—I know only one set of twins. One set who have access to the store and who know it is struggling. One set of twins who think I need to get my life back. It couldn't be them.

Could it?

CHAPTER FOURTEEN

Skylar

I love animals, but the smell of cat urine every day isn't something I enjoy. It's also why I've decided that when I do get my own pet, it's definitely going to be a dog.

"It's about time you got here," a voice I'm not familiar with says. I turn to find my kiss-a- stranger guy, Tyler I believe his name was, smiling with greeting.

"Can I help you?" I ask him.

"No." He chuckles. "I work here. My brother has been filling in for me," he says.

I swap out my coat for one of the long, blue ones I've grown used to wearing while I'm here. It covers every piece of my own clothing so I don't have to worry about ruining the brand-new jeans I bought with my own hard-earned cash. He watches me with a satisfied grin the entire time. From this point on, I'll pretend like that bar night never happened.

"I'm a whole thirty minutes early, in fact," I tell him, grabbing the clipboard off the wall and leaving him in the front room as I head to the back. Once I've fed each animal, I check its feed box; once I wash them, I check their wash box. There's a new sheet every day so I can keep track. Today I'm starting with a Louie, a six-month-old German Shepard, who by the looks of him, he should be at least a year old. This dog grows fast and whines like crazy.

"He only makes that noise when you're around him, so my brother has told me."

I scratch behind Louie's ears.

"How long have you known I work here?"

"Probably since the first day you came in. My brother called to tell me about you."

Tyler is a good-looking guy; he's not as built as Luke, but when he grins at me, it still sends a flutter through my stomach.

"I do give some pretty rad ear scratches," I say, keeping our conversation on the dogs. I clip the leash on Louie's collar and lead him out of his cell. *I probably shouldn't call his kennel a cell out loud.*

"So hey," Tyler says, following behind me. "I know we don't know each other, but I was wondering if you'd like to get dinner." His hands disappear in the front pockets of his jeans as he shrugs. "With me, tonight."

He's asking me out on a date? I could cross off another goal on my to-do list. I mean, I'd go to dinner with him either way, I'm sure, but this lets me multitask. I like to multitask, it turns out. A month ago I didn't have even one thing I had to do each day—now I plan things to fill the whole day.

"Skylar?" Oh, yeah, he's waiting for an answer.

"I'd—"

"Hey, sorry to just …" Luke's words trail off as he notices Tyler. "Sorry, I didn't know you were in here, too."

No one speaks. *So this is what that awkward moment feels like.*

"It's cool, I was just heading back inside," Tyler finally says.

"Oh, but—"

"We can finish this topic later, Skylar. It's not important."

I feel my mouth open into an O as he walks away. Did he just un-ask me out?

"Everything okay?" Luke asks, handing me a plastic bag. His lips are pressed together.

"What?"

Why does he look like he wants to smile but won't?

"What, what?" he asks.

"Stop looking at me like that," I say, feeling my cheeks warm under his gaze.

"What were you two talking about?"

"Nothing."

"Okay, well, in that case, I thought I would—"

"He asked me out, and I was just about to tell him yes when you walked in here like you own this place. How did you get in here anyway?"

"Oh, Mrs. Mulligan and I go way back."

"I'm sure."

"What do you mean, you were going to tell him yes?" His face wrinkles up like the thought alone will make him sick. "We made out last night."

"Well, I didn't hear you asking me out," I say, and his head jerks back. I nod—like, yeah, I told him—and then lead Louie, who has been waiting patiently by my side, around

Luke. I tap the stand where so the dog will jump so I can wash him.

"I'm sorry, I was too busy reacting to the break-in to remember I was supposed to ask you out."

He has a point there.

"You can ask me now."

Where is this bravery coming from, and where in heck was it when I was growing up? I turn the hose on and set it to the shampoo setting. Then I act as cool as I can, when inside I'm freaking out. I just asked him to ask me out. Does this count as making the first move? I could cross that off my list, but then again, kissing him at the bar last night could also count for that one. Either way, it's safe to assume I have accomplished that one.

"I'm still not fully convinced that you aren't the person who is sabotaging my store."

I spray him with the hose. On accident of course, but really, this is a solid response to what he just said.

"How is that possible?" I snap. I'm so sick and tired of him—

Large arms wrap around my waist as he pulls me in. He's all wet now. His shirt is sticking to his chest, and when he presses our bodies together, the water seeps through my coat and into my clothes. Luke shuts off the water, and then he kisses me.

It's nothing like last night. Today his kiss is harder, like he can't resist me. He backs me up against the wall, nudging my legs apart to make room for one of his. If he presses any closer, he's going to be able to feel my heart beating against his own chest.

"I would ask you out, but I specifically remember a line on your list that reads, "ask a guy out.""

"And you think I should ask you out."

"Yep."

Honestly, he'd be the best person to ask out because, as of right now, I have a good hunch he wouldn't say no.

"Luke, will you go out with me?"

"No."

"What? You just said to—"

"No, because a lady should never have to ask a guy out."

I laugh, like I seem to do with him a lot, and give my attention back to Louie.

"If you're not busy tonight, I'd love to spend the evening with you, Sky, on a date."

The use of my nickname and the sincerity in his voice sets my heart into full speed.

"Okay," I say, because we both know I'm going to say yes no matter how long I wait to answer.

"Okay," he says, kisses me quickly, and is gone.

Holy crap. I have a date. Tonight. With Luke. Looks like Tyler un-inviting me was a good thing.

* * *

I can't remember the last time I got ready for a date that I actually wanted to go on. In fact, scratch that, this is the first date I've ever actually wanted to go on. I take one more look in the mirror, smoothing my hands over my dress, and fluff my hair one more time. This is also the most dressed up I've been since I left home.

My reflection catches my attention. I look like the exact

same girl who has always looked back at me, yet on the inside I feel like a whole new person, and I've never felt so light and happy in I can't remember how long.

Knock, knock.

A smile beams back at me.

I grab my purse and open the door, but Luke isn't standing on the other side. There is a rose and note taped to the door, however.

Sky,

Meet me downstairs. You'll know where to find me.

Luke

I smell the rose, inhaling as I descend the stairs. I push the door open slowly. The entire store is glowing by candlelight.

I take in the room, knowing my smile is wide. In the corner I suggested for a reading nook, Luke is standing there in a green polo that's tucked into a pair of dark blue jeans. He's holding the remainder of the rose bouquet in front of him. Behind him sits a burgundy loveseat with one small, white table on each side of it. Exactly as I described it.

"I know I should take you out, spoil you, show you off because I've never seen anyone look as radiant as you do right now, but I also know I'm one lucky guy that you are giving me this chance. I'm selfish and that's why I want to keep you to myself tonight, if that's okay with you."

He takes a step toward me, handing me the flowers. I try to hide my smile behind them as I breathe in their scent. If I can find another facial expression besides a smile tonight, I'll be shocked.

"This is more than okay," I answer him.

His eyes meet mine, and his lips break into the grin I'm growing to love more each day. "What are we having?" I ask, taking in the sight of a plush blanket spread across the floor in front of the sofa.

"Well, I was thinking we could test our new reading corner. See if it's comfortable and a space people would enjoy using." A rosy color takes over his cheeks as he gestures for me to join him on the floor.

"So far so good."

And then an awkward silence falls over us. Without thinking too hard, I grab his face and kiss him. I'm pretty certain this is not the way to go about a first date. But again, nothing about me or us is normal.

Luke

Her fingers slide between mine, and I flip our hands over, pulling up until my lips kiss the back of her hand. I feel her breath as she turns her head at the touch. I don't waste another minute. Removing my hand from hers and placing one on each side of her head, I hold her lips against mine. I feel her moan against my tongue as she sinks into my embrace.

She lifts herself to her knees, pushing me back, and I let her. I've never been with a woman who knows exactly what she wants, and I've been learning the last few days that Sky is someone I misjudged in every way possible.

I remove my hands from hers and run them up the sides of her thighs as she straddles me. Warmth radiates from her and the thin layer between us. My jeans feel tight immediately and, as much as I don't want to stop this, I should. This isn't proper first-date etiquette, and Sky deserves to be treated better.

With my hands on her hips, I hold her still and pull my lips back.

"This is one hell of a way to start a date," I say.

She drops her chin and covers her face with her hands. "I know, I know, this is so bad. I don't do this. But, I … I couldn't take not talking, and then, well, I mean, I wanted to kiss you, and I figured I may as well just do it now instead of—"

I pull one hand from her face and I kiss her. This time though, it's slow and gentle. She makes the choice to end it this time, crawling off of me and rising to sit on the couch.

"I probably should have started with something more like that than just jumping on top of you," she says.

"I'm not complaining," I say, taking the spot next to her.

"But you stopped me."

"Yeah, I don't want you to think I planned this type of date because I assumed you and I would be … physical."

"All right." She smiles at me. "Let's eat."

The blush I saw earlier is back. She takes a deep breath, her chest rising. Dinner can wait. That's what microwaves are for, right?

I place my hands at her waist and lift her in a swift move until she is on top of me again. Her legs slide against my sides as she sits on my lap. Her eyes are wide but not with fear. With excitement and approval. She crashes her mouth to mine.

My hands lose control, roaming over her ass and up her

back. Her dress bunches under my fingertips as I move them to the swell of her breasts. Her knees slide from their spot against my side, causing my hands to drop to her waist. Has she changed her mind? But it's the opposite. By moving her knee, she's spread her legs wider, allowing her to sink closer to the spot where our bodies meet. Her hips begin to move back and forth. Her hands have a firm grip, holding my face as she kisses me harder. Then she moans, and it's the sign I need to know she's all in.

With a hold around her waist, I flip her to her back. Her dress falls to her waist at the same time she lifts her hips for me to glide her panties off. She makes quick work with my belt, pulling it out of the loops effortlessly and tossing it to the floor. Pushing against the sofa to raise myself, Sky tugs my pants down with her foot. Next, she's clawing at my shirt until it comes off.

I've never been undressed so quickly before. There's only one problem. She's still wearing her dress.

I lower my hips to rest between her legs and then kiss her, pulling her back with me as she lifts the dress. Our lips never break except when she pulls the soft fabric over her head. I find the condom that is always in my wallet and slide it on. Her kisses are faster now and more desperate than ever. I've never felt so wanted in my entire life. I place myself at her entrance and then take a moment to look at her. So much desire and happiness is radiating off her. She rolls her eyes when I smile, and I fail at hiding my laugh; she pulls me back down for more kissing. I chose that moment to enter her.

The kissing stops as her head falls back. Her hands grip my ass, and when she squeezes I take that as a sign to speed up.

The sounds of our breathing and the repeated groans and moans as I rock my hips fill the room. It doesn't take much time for us to reach the breaking point together. She never cries out harder, or says my name, or anything else, but when her eyes look in mine, she doesn't have to say anything. I know exactly what she needs. I know this because not once tonight have I thought about the store, not once have I cared about when it will open. All that matters right now is Sky. She needs me, and I'm pretty sure I need her, too.

CHAPTER FIFTEEN

Skylar

I've never been so excited for a holiday, and I don't care that it's only Halloween to everyone else. It's *Halloween* to me.

"If you could pick any costume, what would you be?" Alex asks.

"Like with everything else in your life, I can't believe you have never dressed up for Halloween. I would imagine rich people still have some sort of party," Beth says.

"The closest we ever got was a masquerade ball, and trust me when I say they aren't as fun as you think. The masks are awesome, but keeping them on, being able to see and smile without the mask moving, is such a pain. And in my family, you were always taking pictures no matter what the event, so my mother, Eloisa Atwood, would lose her mind if you smiled and your mask moved and someone decided to use *that* picture."

"So, basically, the rich and famous life is not as glamorous as the movies make it out to be."

I shrug. "I mean, it had its moments." Some of which I know, after living in Wind Valley, I took for granted. Now I'd give anything to go back just to get my trust fund to help Luke with the store.

"What about this nurse costume?" Alex holds up an outfit that, by the looks of the picture on the front of the bag, doesn't cover very much.

I flip it to the back, looking at the price tag. "Fifty dollars for this. I may as well wear my bra and panties to the bar and save myself some cash."

"Luke would die if you did that. Both from wanting to tear your clothes off and to shield you from the view of any other man," Beth jokes as she pulls out a slutty fireman's dress as we make our way down another aisle with costumes for women.

I want my costume to be somewhat realistic. Just because I'm dressing up doesn't mean I have to go full on into the clichéd world of girls wearing the smallest piece of clothing they can find for Halloween.

"Well, what are you two planning to be?" I ask.

"Conner wants to dress up as a couple," Alex answers, and she doesn't sound too excited.

"And I'm not dressing up," Beth says.

"I can totally see Conner being that sort of guy, and, Beth, why not?"

She shrugs and pulls out the next costume. A pink poodle skirt appears from the rack.

"What if you and Luke did a couples costume, too? You could be Sandy and he could be Danny."

"Who and who?" I ask.

Both of their eyes widen, and Alex's mouth opens into a large oval shape.

"You've never seen *Grease*, the movie?" Beth asks. "Please tell me you watched movies before you came here."

I nod, but really I didn't watch very many movies because I was always making appearances for my parents. Or I was at the hair stylist because my mother thought my roots need to be touched up, or my ends were too dry, or because the length of my hair didn't flatter the shape of my face. Or I was doing some silly sport training for tennis or horseback riding, just so my mother could brag about me being the best. Everything was a competition with her.

"I don't believe you," Beth says, opening my purse to pull out my list. She pulls a pen from hers and writes "watch *Grease*" at the bottom. "Luke would die some more if you showed up to work in a pair of leather pants."

"Especially since you've become a very popular bartender over the last couple of weeks. Conner told me you had the same couple come in every night last week and request you."

I smile. My first regulars. It's a silly thought, but it means something to me.

"Did you say leather?" I ask.

"Oh dear Lord, that settles it. We are finding you that Sandy outfit."

"If Luke and I didn't go in a couple's costume, what do you think he would be?" We've been hanging out for a while as more than friends, which I really, *really* enjoy, but there is so much more about him I need to learn. Maybe his costume choice will tell me something.

"Hmm, if it were the old Luke, I'd say he'd show up in a Tarzan outfit," Beth answers.

"Really? I thought he would be more like the type of guy to show up as Picasso or some other painter," says Alex.

"Do you know any other famous painters?" Beth asks.

Alex sticks her tongue out and they laugh. But I'm pretty sure I got lost somewhere.

"Neither of those costumes make sense to me." I shake my head and pause to pull out another costume for consideration. *No.* I don't think I would make a very good gypsy.

"That doesn't surprise me since Luke is just now starting to act like himself. It wouldn't surprise me, either, if he finally starts painting again," Beth says.

"He paints?" I know relationships take time, but painting is something I should know he likes by this point, right?

"Hey, don't look so upset about it. He hasn't done a lot since his dad passed. He stopped doing anything that wasn't work related for his mom and sisters. He'll find his way back, and if you two keep going like you are, you'll be there with him every step of the way," Beth says, giving me a side hug.

I nod. She's right, and I know just how to help him, too.

Screw this Sandy and Danny costume idea. I have an ever better one.

Luke

Class ends early for the weekend, and I head for my car. I want to stop by the bookstore before I head into work so I can kiss on my girl before we have to control ourselves in a room full of people all night. It's been hard to keep my hands off her. Not only is she sexy as hell, she's one of the kindest and most honest people I've ever met. Everything feels calm and right when I'm with her.

I dig my cell from my pocket when it dings and shove it back when I see it's another text from Brandy asking me to come by the house. I've been avoiding my sisters when I can and only going by Mom's when they're in school.

I don't want to think they're the ones who broke in any more than I want to remember how much I blamed Sky for it. I don't want to turn into that person again. And I really don't want to think about how each time I replace the window, this damn inspector guy tells me two weeks. Two weeks. *I just want to open my store already!*

If it were my sisters and I just let it go, what does that say about me? I'd treat a stranger like crap for tearing the place apart, but I'd let my sisters get away with it because they're family? If they did it, there has to be some type of punishment. Right?

My cell buzzes again, but this time, it's Sky.

Sky: Hey I'm putting my costume together with Beth before work. I'll just ride there with her. See you soon. XOXO.

I slump into the driver's seat of my truck. I guess I won't be stopping by the store after all. I should probably just head home and get ready myself. My costume doesn't take much, but until I know exactly what to say to my sisters, keeping clear of them for just a bit longer is best.

* * *

I'm pouring what feels like my hundredth draft beer of only the first hour of the night when a white blob catches my eye. I have to double take. Sky, in a fully white outfit, including a pair of white heels, approaches my end of the counter.

"Hey there," she says with a wink and then continues on as if the tight clothing is normal. I know it's Halloween and I'm the worst for assuming, but I really thought I'd see more skin tonight. I mean, Beth is dressed as Ariel, and where I would think she'd wear those fishnet looking things girls wear, she's displaying her bare legs instead. Abby is wearing —well, that doesn't really apply because she shows a lot of skin every day—but as I take a quick scan around the room, Sky is the only woman wearing pants as the bottom half to her costume.

She passes behind me at the bar, a finger stroking across my back as she goes. That touch—*damn*—makes me really wish we weren't at work right now. I twist slowly, taking in how tight this outfit really is and how perfectly round it shows off her ass. But I have no idea what she is. I'm about to ask when Alex, dressed as Catwoman and the second woman to wear pants so far, cuts me off.

"Hey, Sky." She leans over the counter, handing Sky a bucket with paintbrushes sticking out of it. "You forgot the rest of your costume."

Sky, is now beaming with a smile just as white as her ensemble. Alex laughs as she walks to a table in the back where Sara, Logan, Ethan, and Kelsey are sitting.

"I feel like I should really know what you are by this point, but all I can think is that you're a painter?" I ask as she shrugs off the white jacket and reveals a simple white tank underneath.

"Nope, guess again."

"A famous painter?"

I'm not very good at guessing.

"Nope."

The P pops on her lips, and I have to control myself from touching them with my own. Why do we have to be at work right now?

"I'm a blank canvas," she says.

Wow.

"And I happen to know a painter"—she leans in—"who might enjoy a blank canvas"—she leans in farther, her lips almost touching my ear—"to paint. Alone. Tonight."

I'm pretty sure everyone in the bar just heard the bob in my throat.

"And if he gets too messy, I guess I'll just give him a nude canvas instead."

Yup. Yes. And now I'm severely annoyed that we are at work.

"Hello, paper towel boy, I need my drinks," Abby interrupts.

I roll my eyes.

"I'm the Brawny Man," I say, shooting Sky a wink. I step to pass her and wrap my fingers around her wrist, pulling her close to whisper in her ear. "Our first painting will definitely be messy."

I leave her standing with a satisfied look on her face as I get to work. This is about to be the longest, but then best, night of my life.

Skylar

Luke dropped me off and told me he'd be back in less than ten minutes. So, in my genius idea to use the heat already brewing inside me to ignite him the moment he steps through the door—and because I've always wanted to do this—I strip naked and crawl onto the bed. I'll be the first thing he sees when he walks through the door. All of me.

I attempt a few different poses to choose which I think is the best. I decide on the one with me on my belly, legs bent, ankles crossed, and looking back at him over my shoulder.

I get into position right as the door opens. He freezes. He doesn't make any facial expressions, but his chest moves quickly as his eyes rack my entire body.

"Sky, you look … wow."

He strides to one side of the bed, setting a few small, white cups on the nightstand. They each have splashes of paint in them. He brought paint. He *really* brought paint. My heart thuds as I watch him get out three different brushes, dipping each into a different color. *Holy smokes, he's going to paint me.*

"I'm so glad you're ready for me," he says, swirling the brush in one cup. "But I think you should flip over. Tonight, I think I'll start with the front."

Without thinking about it, I flip over. My arms are glued to my sides as I lay stiff.

"Relax." His deep chuckle sends goose bumps all over my skin. But I do relax, because he's grinning at me, and I love that grin.

Hovering one brush over my body, he slowly drips color from my chest to my ribs to my belly button. My back arches when the cold paint touches me where I want him most.

"Hold still," he says. He grabs another color, repeating

this process up and down my legs. He takes the last color, continuing the process over my entire body this time. He pauses over my breasts.

He leans in, his lips tugging on my ear. "Close your eyes," he whispers.

I do.

I inhale at the first drop of paint. The next drop hits my right nipple, and I jerk forward. Luke's hand gently presses me back to the mattress. Another drop to my left nipple makes me cry out.

"Luke, stop teasing me, please."

"Baby, this isn't teasing. This," he pauses, "is teasing."

A brush touches my chest and slowly, agonizingly, Luke strokes across one breast, then the other. Down to my stomach, and farther. I squirm with desire each time the soft bristles touch a new spot of my body. I'm wet, all over, and I love it. I want Luke more than anything right now.

His movements have slowed, and I hear the zipper of his pants. Then clothes shuffling. I peek with one eye and easily spot how much this is turning him on, just like me.

"Keep those eyes closed, Sky. Or I'll do only this all night," he laughs.

I squeeze my eyes shut and try to gain some type of control over my body. I just want to yank that paintbrush out of his hand, throw it across the room, and pull him into me.

My attention goes to the bristles again as the near my core. Closer and closer.

"Take a deep breath," he says just as I think the bristles are about to touch me there. Instead, I feel him push into me, and even though my eyes are closed, I see stars. The wonderful feeling of him filling me is more than I can handle.

I lock my arms around his neck, holding on. He lowers himself until we are chest to chest, the paint smearing between us. He grips the back of my legs, bending them to his sides, and then he runs his hands over the paint he left there and on my chest, rubbing it over my skin. The easy glide of each touch makes him thrust faster, harder. My ankles lock around him, holding him in place as my orgasm crashes through my body.

"Sky," Luke calls out as he slows. He presses his lips against mine and rides out the last of his own release. "I think I just fell in love with painting all over again."

We both glance down at the yellow, blue, and green swirls of paint that cover us and laugh. It's on my sheets, comforter, and pillows.

"This mess—totally worth it," I tell him and kiss him again.

Life is so much better than I ever thought it could be.

CHAPTER SIXTEEN

Skylar

I wake to the soft tickles of Luke's fingers over my back. Last night was the first night he's ever slept over. I could get used to waking this way. That grin he's giving me—yeah, that's pretty nice to wake up to as well.

"You should really take a shower," he says.

And that, I do not want to wake up to.

"Good morning to you, too."

I sit up, pulling the covers with me to cover myself as I lean against the wall. Luke's chuckle goes right to my core as he copies my position.

"I only say that because there is paint all over the bed and you." His eyes slowly take in the parts of me still uncovered. The way his eyes gaze at the blanket as though he can see right through it makes my heart beat fast.

"Oh" is the only thing I come up with for a response.

"And as much as I'd love to join you, I have to get downstairs. The inspector should be here anytime." He crawls out of bed, pulling on a pair of blue jeans and tugging a charcoal t-shirt over his head. "All I need is for him to give me the green light and tomorrow, Warren Books will be back open for business."

"Finally," I say. "You'll have to let me know when you want me to work, you know, to pay for rent."

"I don't know if that's still a requirement to live here, but I'm not going to argue if you want to work in the store, especially with the holidays. I won't be able to hire someone new right away anyhow." He kisses the top of my head. "Oh, on that subject, I'm not sure what you had planned for Thanksgiving, but would you want to—and I get it if you don't because you do have your own family and all—but would you want to, um—"

"I'd love to have Thanksgiving with you and your family, of course, if that's what you're trying to ask me."

He smiles and nods. "I'll meet you downstairs when you're ready. We can go to breakfast when the inspector is done."

"Sounds perfect."

A smile is glued to my face as he leaves.

When the door latches closed, I whip the sheet off and rush to the bathroom. I shower in record time, twist my hair into a bun, apply a light bit of makeup, and put on an outfit very similar to Luke's. I'm bouncing down the stairs after thirty minutes, total, the same goofy smile on my face as before.

"Since when is that required?" Luke's loud voice carries into the stairwell as I reach the door to the store.

"It's always been code. Somehow, your father must have gotten around it, but I won't sign off on this until it's fixed."

"That's going to take me weeks and cost me more money than I can afford to spend on the store right now."

"I'm sorry, Luke, but you can't have extension cords running everywhere. You'll have to install more outlets. I don't make the rules, just enforce them. And the shelves are too close together." He pauses and I take this moment to step into the room. "They need to be thirty-six inches apart, not thirty-three. There isn't enough room to fit a wheelchair down each aisle. And there should forty inches of room at the end of aisle to turn."

The inspector rips said sheet off of his clipboard and hands it to Luke.

"Call me when it's ready, and I'll be back to sign off for you."

Luke doesn't say anything to him as he walks out the door. The room falls silent enough to hear every breath he takes.

I take a slow, hesitant step toward Luke. He crunches the sheet of paper into a ball and tosses it to the floor.

"I don't have the time to deal with this. I can't do it all anymore."

I lick my lips and look away. Just seeing the pain in his eyes chokes me up.

"Luke, it's going to be okay. We'll get things fixed and open this place up in no time."

"It could be another month, maybe more. Where am I going to get the money?"

"We just need to make a few phone calls and get—"

"Oh, what do you know?" he growls. "You have no idea what it feels like to bust your ass to provide for someone. To take care of family. You had everything you needed and you left it behind for what? To prove a point."

I stand frozen. I can feel the prickling of tears at the back of my eyes. My teeth hurt as I grind them together. He doesn't know what he's talking about. He's angry, and I'm the only one here for him to take his anger out on.

"What, you don't have anything to say?"

I let out a breath, slowly. "I'm not going to argue with you when you're this upset. I care about you too much to say something I will regret later."

"Mad, Skylar? I'm fucking furious. I should have put more time into this place instead of picking up shifts at the bar. I should have dropped the entire semester to give this place my full attention. I shouldn't have …" His eyes meet mine and he doesn't finish that sentence. "Every day you watch me struggle with this goddamned place just so I can reopen. You say you care about me, but that's a lie. If you cared, you would have offered to help take this burden away by now."

Wow.

Okay, now I have something to say.

"So, what you're saying is, because my family comes from money I should just offer it to you because we're together?"

"Skylar—"

"That even though you're fully aware I came here to build my own life and make my own way, I should just give it all up because you're struggling."

My own voice is beginning to scare me.

"Skylar—"

"How dare you think I owe you anything! Are you even with me because you want to be, or is it because you want my family's money? Is that what you were trying to say, that you shouldn't have wasted your time with me?"

"Sky—"

"Because, news flash, Luke! I have no money! It was never my money to begin with. I can't help you. *Sorry* to let *you* down."

I march for the door to the stairwell. *Screw him.* I've spent too much time in my life with men who think money is everything.

"Sky, wait."

I jerk open the door, not slowing to listen to him. Luke comes up behind me, grabs my wrist to stop me, and turn me around. I have to cross my arms to control myself from reaching up and slapping him. I can't even look at him right now.

"I'm *so* sorry. I don't even know why I said that. I wasn't thinking."

I'm not saying anything.

"I didn't mean any of it. I swear to God I didn't. I should have calmed down before I spoke. You've done nothing but support me, even when I accused you of breaking in. You've believed in me and the store. I know you care. I care about you, and nothing else. I don't care about this store. I don't care about the money. Tell me you forgive me. Please, Sky. Tell me I didn't just mess this all up."

Ugh! I can't just pretend like he didn't hurt me. And I can't pretend that I believe him. Money is important to him. It always will be. At this point, I just don't know how much.

"I think … I think we should just get some space … for a bit."

"But—"

"Please, Luke."

He drops his hold on my arm, and I head up the stairs. When I reach the top, I glance over my shoulder. Luke is still standing at the bottom. He's holding the door open with his hand hanging in front of him.

Defeat, yeah, I'm feeling it too. I lock myself in my apartment, thankful I don't work tonight. It means I don't have to come out for the rest of the day.

Luke

I couldn't sleep last night. I kept envisioning Sky's face when I yelled at her.

I can't believe I said all that to her. I've never even thought 90 percent of the shit that came out of my mouth. I mean, I wouldn't have taken the money if she offered it. I go on and on about the value of hard work; taking the money would be wrong for so many reasons. School, yeah, I probably should have taken time off. I don't go to class half the time because I'm with Sky or at the store. The shifts at the bar —okay, I've thought about that decision too, but only because I started to make time for myself, I missed it and wanted more. But Sky ... god, I don't know if I'll ever be able to show her how wrong I was. But I have to start somewhere, and that's why I'm walking up to Mom's door now.

Okay.

I'm going to do it. I'm going inside and just ask them. For me, but mostly for Sky. She deserves the truth.

God, I'm such a dick.

I'll be calm and understanding if my sisters did it, and if not, then I'll expect the screaming teenage anger that comes from accusing them of something they didn't do. Girls are forgiving for that kind of stuff, aren't they? I could be setting a new record on how fast you can turn every woman in your life against you.

I open the door quietly, hoping to get in a few words with Mom before Brandy and Shea find me. I want to be able to go to them. I want to get the first word in.

"Luke, I wasn't expecting you to come by today." Mom smiles over the top of her book from the couch. The book cover is different than the last book I saw in her hands. Mom's always been a reader. According to my dad, that was one of the reasons he was so drawn to her.

"I actually came by to talk to the twins. Are they home?"

"Upstairs, watching a movie last I saw them," she says. "Is everything okay, Luke?"

"Yeah, of course."

"And Sky, how is she?"

I feel my face practically break in two at the fake smile I give her. "She's good." Lying to Mom feels like I'm being kicked in the heart, but she doesn't need to be loaded down with my problems.

"I hope you'll bring her over for Thanksgiving next week."

"I'll ask her, but she might have plans or be going home. We haven't talked about it," I say and then turn for the stairs. More lies. Yeah, I asked Sky. But the chances she will still come aren't looking good.

"Luke, have I ever told you about how your father and I met?" Mom asks.

"Yeah, you were working in the store, and he couldn't get

you to leave him alone." I laugh, remembering Dad's shortened version of the story. Mom laughs, too.

She closes her book and sets it on the table.

"But did we ever tell you about the first, very first, time we met?"

I sit down, sensing there is going to be more than a short version to the story. I shake my head.

"Well, I was seventeen, just a few weeks shy of my birthday, and I was mad. Mad that my parents had just told me they couldn't afford to buy me a gift that year. That would make the third year that money kept me from a gift. I should have accepted it, but I couldn't." She smiles. "I was walking past the bookstore when a blue cover caught my eye. I couldn't stop looking at it. It was both bright and soft at the same time. The big white letters of the title looked like clouds in the sky. I wanted that book."

She scoots close to me and pats me on the knee as she laughs.

"I saw your dad behind the counter when I went in, and I asked him if he could find me a book. I can't tell you what book I asked for, but he got up and went to the back to see if they had it. When he came back out, I was almost through the front door with that blue book.

"He yelled and chased me about half a block. And then he dragged me by the arm to face his father, and I tell you, Luke, I was more terrified of that man than I was thinking about how I had to tell my own parents what I'd done.

"Your grandfather must have taken pity on me though, after I broke down and told him why I did it. Then he made me a deal. He told me that on my eighteenth birthday I should come back to the store and fill out paperwork to be an employee. He'd give me a job, an apartment to live in, and a store full of books I could read anytime. Then he told your father that if he'd had as much passion as I did for even just one book, maybe he'd be able to own the store one day."

She looks up, tears filling her eyes, and I hug her. Still a bit lost on why she is telling me this, but I won't dare tell her that.

"Your father hated that store. Hated it every day of his life. But he kept it because he knew it made me happy. How he fell in love with me will never be my story to tell, but your story Luke, you still have time to write it. And if selling the store is really what you want to do, I won't stand in your way."

I lean back. "How did you know about that?"

"The bank called, said they couldn't reach you, and wanted to know if you were able to get the inspector to come out."

"Wow, Mom, I'm sorry. I really wish I'd have been the one to tell you."

"Me, too, but it's okay. Now, go talk to your sisters about what they've done."

"Wait, what?" I stand and glare up the stairs where I find Brandy and Shea sitting on the top step watching us. They're both crying and avoiding any eye contact with me.

"You knew?" I ask Mom.

"Well, when you wouldn't answer their calls, they came to me to ask what they should do. I told them to wait till you came to them."

"So you did do it?" I ask, turning to look at their tear-streaked faces. My voice booms in the silent room, causing Shea to jump.

Slowly, they nod.

"You let me treat Sky like she was a thief. You let her take the blame for you. Why would you do that to another person? You don't get to decide who takes the blame for a choice you made. What happened wasn't her fault, and she shouldn't ever be treated like …" I don't even care about the store anymore.

I swallow, but it's dry and forced as I stand and start for the door. *I should really take my own advice sometimes.*

"Luke, where are you going?" Mom asks.

"I have to do something."

"Wait!" she yells, and I stop. They get five minutes, tops. I have to talk to Sky. Soon.

"We didn't want you to give your life up for that place like Dad did," Brandy says after Mom nods for her to continue the conversation I'm ready to walk out on.

"We just wanted you to be happy, and we thought if the store was gone, you could be you again. Not the guy who thinks he has to take care of everyone," Shea says. "You thought it was Sky, and we thought that would … I don't know."

"We didn't think Skylar would stick around. Then she did and you started to date her and we didn't know what to do." Brandy sighs, leaning her head onto Shea's shoulder.

I pause, trying to come up with something to say. "You should have said something. Just told someone, anyone." My tone is much lighter than before.

"Luke, we just want our brother back. We're sorry," Shea says.

"I'm right here. I didn't go anywhere. I'm the person I've always been."

Almost.

"No," they all say in unison, including my mother.

"You're you now. Love will do that to a person," Mom says and picks up her book. I look back to my sisters, who give me their best attempt at a smile before they both apologize. I don't know how to respond though because I'm not thinking about what they did anymore.

Love.

Am I in love? With Sky?

I head straight for the door, not saying another word. I may not know where I'm going once I'm in my truck, but I know one thing for sure, I *am* in love with Skylar. I don't even need to question it. I love her. Hopefully, I'm not too late.

CHAPTER SEVENTEEN

Skylar

I freaking hate men. Hate. The runner-up to hating men? Money. I hate money just as much.

"Whoa, girl, you pedal any faster and the wheel may actually come off that bike, defeating the whole stationary point of it."

I slow my movements. Beth is right. I was pedaling out my frustration.

"My bad," I say as she goes back to her browsing through her magazine.

You know what else makes me even madder? That part of me that still wants to go to Luke. To pretend he said none of what he really said. To go back to how it was. Mack and I disagreed so many times, but how *I* felt then never mattered. Would Luke care about what I think?

"Okay, you're doing it again. So, please, do spill what has got you so worked up."

"It's nothing," I say. Luke and I should work out our problems. Just us. No one else.

"What did Luke do?"

I stop pedaling.

"How do you know he did something?"

"All my friends have been heartbroken at some point. I know the look."

"Oh, well, it's nothing really. We just need to talk it out."

Yeah, exactly. See, I just needed to say it out loud.

"Sky."

Beth's magazine goes in the air and my hand flies to my heart at the sound of Luke's voice.

"Whoa, Luke, you can't just sneak up on girls like that." Beth rises from her bike to retrieve her magazine. I can see her from the corner of my eye. Luke, though, isn't looking anywhere but at me. I shush my fluttering heart and silently tell my lips to stay tight. No matter how excited I am to see him, I will not show it.

"Clearly now is the time you two are going to talk. So I'll just head to the locker room ... bye ... anyone? ... No one wants to say good-bye? Okay, fine." I hear every word Beth says, but I can't speak. Not with the intensity of Luke's pleading gaze.

He swallows and looks away.

"Can we go outside? I could walk you back to the store while we talk."

"Okay."

I quickly clean my machine and grab my bag from the locker room, where I don't see Beth. When I reach the front doors to the gym, Luke reaches for my bag.

"I'm so incredibly sorry, Sky."

I nod but keep looking straight ahead as we head down the sidewalk. "I know."

"You know I would never use you for money, right?"

I let out a puff of air and shrug. "Nothing is ever a sure thing."

"Sky, I wouldn't. I swear."

"You say that now, but your views could change."

"They won't."

"You don't know that."

"You're right, I don't. I also don't know if one day you could realize that this life, with me, isn't good enough for you and you might leave."

"Have you not heard anything I've said to you? I came here to find myself, Luke; I'm not going back."

"You say that now, but you could always change your mind," he says my words cautiously.

"All right," I say, pausing my step to look up at him. "Now what do we do?"

"We have to trust each other."

He takes one of my hands in his and laces our fingers together.

"It's that easy?" I ask.

"No," he answers, leaning down to kiss the top of my head before we resume walking. "But if you want to be with me as much as I want to be with you, we have to at least try, right?"

I nod, finally letting the smile I'd been holding in free. Luke stops us, wrapping our entwined hands behind my back as he leans in to kiss me before we keep walking

He kisses me good-bye at the door.

We survived our first argument. *I should have had that on my list.* He said he'd never use me, but he needs money to bring this store back to life. What would I do if he ever did ask me to loan him money? Would I do it? Would I go back to that life for Luke?

I'm just about to step through the door when the sun flashes a glare in front of my face. I glance in that direction to see a shiny Lincoln town car driving away. Every piece of the car—the windows, handles, rims, everything—is matte black. Just the way Mack likes his cars.

The car stops. I wait. Then it turns and is gone.

I shake my head. I'm just overthinking things. I must have had hating men on my mind so much I'm seeing things. And right now, the only thing I should be seeing is which outfit I'm going to wear to Thanksgiving. Even if it's three weeks away.

CHAPTER EIGHTEEN

Skylar

I've met Luke's mom a bunch of times. But for some reason tonight seems much more important than all those other times. And this is a holiday. Is she going to be mad that I'm intruding on their family? I could have stayed at the apartment. I mean, any place is better that my parents' house, so I—

"Why is your leg bouncing so much?" Luke asks. I'm aware it hasn't stopped bouncing since he picked me up. In my old life, I never worried what people thought of me. My parents had groomed me to be the perfect daughter. I didn't have to worry about the choices I made because everyone else made them for me. I never did the wrong thing because I was never in a place to make the wrong choice. What if my choices now aren't good enough for her? What if she tells me I'm not good enough for Luke? Luke clearly has had doubts. Will his mother?

I take a deep breath. I'm not that girl anymore, and I like

who I am now better than who I was. She'll like me because I like me.

"I'm sorry. I'll stop bouncing it. The nerves are getting to me."

"But you've met my mom before." He reaches over to squeeze my hand.

"Yeah, I know, but not as your girlfriend."

"You're my girlfriend?" he asks, his whole body sitting up straighter in his seat as he grins at me.

Shoot. Am I? Great, now I'm assuming things, and I'm going to ruin this dinner before we even get there. What do I do? I can't back out now. What would the new me do?

"Yes, I am."

Ohmygod! I can't believe I just did that. I love it. Wait—he shouldn't be frowning.

"What?" I couldn't have misjudged us that badly. He was just smiling three seconds ago.

"Nothing. I just thought, I don't know, I would bring you flowers and ask you like we were in high school or something."

"Oh."

He's so cute.

"I mean, you should have done that weeks ago, but you still can if you want," I joke.

His head falls back to meet the headrest as he laughs. "I just might, but I kind of like the idea that you wanted to be my girlfriend so badly you just decide to call yourself that."

I swat his arm. "Don't make jokes right now."

He chuckles.

I'm two seconds away from asking if his sisters are okay with me coming to dinner when we pull into the single-car driveway of a small, brown house. The driveway is uneven and the white trim on the house is chipped in a few spots, but still, whoever lives here has done what they can to keep up the outside appearance.

Luke walks around the car, opening my door for me.

"Try not to let the first glance of Mom's house give you any impression of her. I know it's not anything close to how you lived before."

He turns for the house, locking his hand with mine, but I tug him back.

Cupping my hand over his cheek until I know he's looking at me and really listening, I say, "I'm not judging anyone. And that isn't my life, Luke. I don't compare anything or *anyone* to where I came from."

It stings my heart that he would even consider it enough to say something to me.

His eyes close right before he kisses me. "I know. I'm not sure why I even said that." He wraps his arms around me. "Let's get inside. It's getting cold out."

With his arms around me, we walk side by side to the door. His mother opens it, greeting us with a big smile as we take the last step. "I'm so happy you could make it."

Luke pulls his mom in for a hug, and when he releases her, she pulls me into an embrace as well.

"I'm so absolutely thrilled to have you here this evening, Sky. It's going to be the first of many, I hope."

"I hope so, too." *I hope Luke and I have a lot of firsts together.*

"Girls! Girls!" His mother shouts up the stairs as Luke closes the door behind us and takes my jacket.

"My sisters, they uh … they want to talk to you before we

eat." Luke flashes me a tight smile and then glances up the stairs behind his mother. He stuffs his hands in his pockets and stares at the floor. Two mini images of his mother come down the steps. They're staring at me with the same smile Luke just gave me.

He continues to look elsewhere, and his mother is points to the living room. "Let's all sit down, shall we?"

All three Warren children move swiftly for the couch.

Why are they all acting so weird?

I take a seat in the open recliner and wait. If I had known I was going to make everyone this awkward, I'd have stayed at the apartment and just waited for Luke to finish his dinner. But I also want them to like me, so I have to do something.

"So, Luke tells me you both play volleyball," I say, hoping to initiate some type of happy conversation. But it doesn't work. One of them starts to cry, and the other just keeps staring at me.

"No to the volleyball?" I have no idea what just happened.

"We did it. It was us," one of the girls says between sobs.

"We are so sorry," the other says.

"Shea, Brandy, let's pull ourselves together and explain what you're talking about," Luke's mom says. "Shea"—she touches the crying girl's hand—"why don't you go first?"

She nods and then looks at me with her red-rimmed eyes. The devastation in her eyes makes my heart beat so hard, I feel like it's about to jump up my throat.

"Brandy and I were the ones who broke into the bookstore," she says, looking away once the words are out. "We didn't think anyone was around and then you were there and we didn't say anything."

They did it and let people believe it was me?

"We thought," Brandy begins, "that if the store was gone, Luke wouldn't have so much to focus on and he could be our brother again."

My hand covers my heart as I look at Luke. He still isn't looking at me.

I know I should be upset, but it's clear from everyone who knew Luke before his father passed away that he was a whole different person back then. His friends and family miss him. His family committed vandalism to get their brother back.

The tears start before I can control them.

"Excuse me," I say, rising and turning for some other place to be right now.

"Bathroom is down the hall on the right," their mother says.

I don't waste time getting there. I'm just about to close the door and lock myself in when a hand pushes the door open. Luke forces his way in and shuts the door behind him.

"Sky, I am so sorry. So crazy sorry." He kisses my forehead as I cry into his chest. He chants "I'm sorry" over and over as I hold on to him. He has nothing to be sorry for. I know he hates how he treated me. He'll feel the guilt for a long time. But I'm not crying because of all that.

I'm crying because he has the family I've always wanted.

"And I'm so sorry I can't seem to say anything other than 'I'm sorry' when things go wrong. I keep messing up, and I—"

"Luke," I say, pulling away and sitting on the edge of the tub.

"Yes, anything. What can I do?" He kneels in front of me, clasping my hands in his.

"You're not messing up, but we do need to pull ourselves together."

"I know."

"Every time you apologize, you do it because you think you did something wrong, and every time that happens, I think, 'Did he do something wrong?'"

"I know."

"Your family would do anything to have you in their lives, Luke. I'm right there with them, if we stop having our doubts."

"Is that why you're crying? Because you have doubts about us?" He swipes away a tear and kisses the spot where it fell.

I shake my head.

"I'm crying because my family hasn't tried to reach out to me. Not once. I knew they wouldn't, and I wanted to leave, but it still hurts, knowing they don't care enough to even try."

"Sky, I'll never be able to make up for your family, but you have me now. I'll do whatever it takes to show you that I'll never leave you."

Luke lips are soft and gentle when he kisses me. I pull him closer and he pushes my knees apart to lean between them and wrap his arms around my waist.

"I want very badly to keep kissing you, but I can smell that turkey and I'm going to need all the energy I can get for the things I plan to do to you tonight."

"Sounds like a perfect idea to me."

With one more kiss, he takes my hand and pulls me to my feet. I stop by the mirror to fix my makeup.

"Should I have my mom ground my sisters?" he asks. "Or should we do something more extreme?"

I laugh.

"It's time to let it go. Let's just get back to us and being happy."

He presses his lips to the top of my head. "I can do that."

His mother and sisters are waiting for us at the table when we return. I take the seat next to Shea. It's clear she's still upset.

"Thank you for telling me the truth," I say to her and Brandy. "Now, who's hungry?"

We each take turns loading our plates with turkey, mashed potatoes, green bean casserole, red-hot applesauce, and so much more. I help his mother and sisters with the dishes after dinner, and before I know it, it's close to midnight and time for us to leave.

My first real family Thanksgiving was a success.

Luke

I feel worse over the entire break-in thing. I mean, I should, definitely. But to Sky, she was just happy the truth was out. That was all she wanted. It never came up, and I'm glad it didn't, but the second break-in wasn't my sisters. It's been a couple months so I think whoever was having their fun is done now. At least, I hope they are. I don't like the idea of Sky living up there alone. Sharing that bit of information isn't something I want to do. I don't want to alarm her.

I lock the door to the bookstore and turn to face Sky. That moment she gives me a push. My back hits the door and my hands fly up like they always do when I feel the need to defend myself, except this time I don't. Just when I am convinced she's going to vent over everything that happened with my sisters, she doesn't. Instead, she presses her lips against mine and rubs her body against me. With each stroke of her tongue, her body moves, touching me in a different place and sending a warm tingle throughout every inch of me.

I wrap my arms around her waist, forcing her body even closer than it already is. My hands slide over her hips and around to her ass. They grip tightly once before moving to the back of her thigh. I lift her, wrapping her legs around me. When I feel her heels lock in the dip of my back, I head for the steps.

Her hands are holding my face in place as she kisses me harder, more frantically. She nips at my bottom lip when I'm halfway up the steps, causing me to take the rest two at a time.

Her door is unlocked, and it slams against the back wall when I push it open. I don't bother to close it since if anyone were to come through the door, they would have to pass through the store first. And I know that door is locked. No one should be bothering us tonight.

We let go of each other as I reach the bed, and she plops down onto the mattress. She laughs and starts stripping off her clothes. I do the same. The more skin she reveals, the more ready I am to explode. Once all our clothes are on the floor, I kneel onto the bed and crawl over her. I nudge one knee between hers and then the other. Then I press on them, opening her legs for me. She begins to push herself higher on the bed, but I grasp her hips and slide her down until she falls perfectly beneath me, my erection pressed against her warm center.

"Luke, you're killing me here," she says, her head digging into the pillows.

"Well, this would be the best way to die, wouldn't it?"

She smirks, and her eyes go to my lips. Reaching up, she pulls me in for a kiss. With the first swoop of her tongue, I push into her. When she breaks the kiss to moan, I pull back.

Desperate eyes meet mine, and she kisses me again. It's more rushed and each time our tongues collide, I thrust into her. When the pressure of her lips against mine becomes harder, so does my movement against her. When her hands start to roam over my back, her nails digging into my skin, I pick up the pace.

"Fuck," I breathe, feeling the sensation for my own release building.

"Don't stop," she begs as she locks her legs around me. I reach between us and rub my finger over her as I pump. Harder and faster. One, two, three, and we come together.

As our heart rates return to a somewhat normal pace, I pull out of her and curl her into me. She rests her head on my bicep, brushing her lips against it after each breath. I kiss the back of her head.

I have the feeling we won't be getting much sleep tonight. And I'll be okay with having nothing ever again if it means I get to have Sky in my life. For the first time since my father's death, I finally feel like everything in life is falling into place.

* * *

Sky's breathing returns to normal while I feather kisses over her face, down her neck, and over her chest.

"I told the bank I wasn't selling anymore," I say when her bright eyes look up at me in the morning light.

"You did?"

"I want to make sure you know what you were getting into."

"I'm fully aware of the choices I've been making, and I'm about 99 percent sure that you like them, too."

Pushing me back, Sky climbs on top of me, kissing my neck.

"So now we just have to prove that we trust the other."

I lift her chin so I can kiss her lips. "I believe in us. We can do it."

When she goes in for another kiss, I, unfortunately, have to pull back.

"As much as I would enjoy continuing this, I have to get to campus to go over my schedule next semester with my advisor." I need to sign up for art classes next semester. It's time I get things back on track. And I want to make sure I'm signed up before all the spots are taken.

With a sigh, she falls back to her side of the bed.

"All right. I guess I did tell Mrs. Mulligan I would stop back by this afternoon since Tyler is going to be gone for a few days."

"He still volunteers there too?"

"Yes, and you have nothing to worry about. He knows we're together."

"An exclusive relationship hasn't stopped him before." *Although I hope he learned his lesson.*

"Seriously?" she asks, rising from the bed and tugging on a pair of jeans.

"Yeah, he and Kelsey dated before she and Ethan got together."

"Really?" Her eyes widen as she combs through her hair

in the mirror and pulls it into a high ponytail. "This really is a small town, isn't it?"

"Almost too small."

Once we're both dressed, we bundle up in our coats, as the weather is growing colder, and we head in the direction of the shelter and the college.

I graze my pinky against Sky's as she locks our hands together. A breeze blows a plastic bag through the park, stealing my attention.

"I don't like the idea that you were living out here," I say, squeezing her hand.

"It wasn't as bad as I'm sure it sounds."

"You had no place to go … I just wish I'd known. Maybe I could have given you a job at the store or a place to live."

"You would have done that for a girl you didn't know?"

His lips pucker to the side before he answers. "I would have at least told Beth to do something about it."

We both laugh.

"Beth would have been all over it. She would have never let me hear the end of it, either."

"No, she wouldn't have, but maybe we could have started dating sooner."

"Or maybe, had you known, we'd never have dated," she says.

She could be right. I like to think that the two of us would have gotten together no matter what happened in our lives, but I know that's not true. I knew she hung out with our friends and I'd done nothing about it until I was forced.

"I'll see you tonight?" I ask once we reach the shelter. I work tonight, but she doesn't and I hope she is cool with me coming back to her place when I get off.

"Of course," she says with a kiss. "We have to pick up where we just left off, remember?"

This time I pull her in for a deeper kiss, our tongues dancing together as we make out on the street outside the shelter where the town gossip queen is probably sitting inside watching us. I don't care. Let her tell every person she knows. Sky is with me, and I'm the luckiest guy in the world.

CHAPTER NINETEEN

Luke

I set the tray of White Russians on the counter and grab Beth's attention to get the drinks her table ordered. With Sky and me on the right track again, I actually feel less stressed. If I focus on one thing as a time, I'll be fine even without selling the store. It will always be there. Skylar, though—I'll find a way to show her how much she means to me.

The door opens as a new customer arrives, someone I don't recognize. He stands tall and adjusts his tie as he surveys the bar. Another man, looking like his exact clone, walks in behind him. From the way he stops behind him, it's clear that man number one calls the shots for this duo. His head turns slowly, and I can't seem to find something, anything else to look at.

When his gaze finds me behind the bar, I swear it's like the man grows another inch or two taller. His eyes narrow as they continue to focus on me. Clearly, my looking at him has pissed him off.

"Luke," Beth nudges me. "Do you know who that is?"

"No," I answer, thankful she was able to draw my focus to something else. I ask the man in front of me if he needs another beer, and he nods. I turn to pull a bottle from the fridge, and the feeling that this stranger in the bar is watching me never leaves. I twist the cap off harder than needed and set it on the counter. Beer sloshes over the top. I'm about to apologize for spilling the customer's drink, but the man isn't sitting there anymore. He's been replaced by the man who is clearly here for me. I just don't know why.

"Be a doll and take this disgusting drink out of my face and deliver it to the unwashed man who has moved seats." He directs his request toward Beth. She huffs.

I toss my towel to the counter behind me and cross my arms. *Who the fuck is this jackass?*

"Can I help you with something?" I ask. Beth takes the beer. I keep my eye on her as she walks around the side of the bar. The guy in front of me who has shit for brains isn't sitting, and if he so much as thinks about messing with Beth, I'll be over this counter top so fast he won't even have a chance to blink.

Beth sets the drink down and moves on to take another table's order. She glances at me, and I nod. *I can handle this jackass.*

"I'll take a scotch, neat."

I lean back, folding my arms in front of me.

"I asked if there was something I could help you with. Making you a drink isn't an option."

"But this is a bar, yes? And that is what you do here, yes?"

"Not for people like you."

"Is that so? I would imagine that when a man like me

walks in here, clearly with money and ready to spend it, everyone in this place would beg to wait on me."

"You're mistaken."

"Am I, *Luke*?"

I try to remain calm. How the fuck does this dickweed know who I am? But I'm pretty sure the moment my jaw ticks and a satisfied grin hits his face, I'm reacting exactly as he planned.

"If I'm not mistaken, you need money. You need a *great deal* of money, actually."

His left brow raises, waiting for my response. I don't bite.

"All right, I see how it is. I am a businessman willing to make a deal with you. This deal will provide you, your mother, and your sisters with enough money that you can all go back to the happy family you were before such tragedy found you. Enough money that you can make all your dreams come true, Luke—you can keep the bookstore and paint and even travel to all those places you've wanted to see. I can give you all that."

He leans back as if everything he just said has won me over. He's wrong. I don't care how much money this guy has; whatever he is offering, I don't want it. What I do want is for him to forget he knows anything about my family.

"That offer sounds great and all, but I'll pass. You can see yourself out." I walk away, ready to be done with this conversation. An alarm system would be a good investment for my mom and sisters.

A closed fist slams down on the counter, stopping me and gaining the attention of the entire bar. Conner excuses himself from the customer he is speaking with, and out of the corner of my eye I see Beth grab Abby's arms, stalling her from coming this direction. I hold my hand up, stopping Conner too. I can handle this guy, and based on what he knows about me, the fewer people I bring into this, the better. I have nothing to hide, but did my father?

"You will take my offer," he seethes.

"It's time for you to leave," I say in a low voice.

"I'm not leaving this town without my fiancé. She will come home with me, and you are going to make that happen."

"Sorry, pal, but I don't know anything about a fiancé. You must have the wrong guy."

"Unless Skylar Atwood is fucking another man besides you, I'm talking to exactly who I need to be talking to."

He knows Sky? Is he saying she's his fiancé?

"Oh, she never told you. She's engaged. To me. The name's Mack, Mack Johnson."

I take a deep breath and feel my teeth grind together.

"She may be sleeping with you now," Mack continues, "but the next bed she's going to be in is mine, and—"

He doesn't have a chance to finish whatever it is he was going to say. His fancy suit is curling into my grip as I launch myself over the counter and drag him to the door. He's tripping the entire way, yelling for someone to "pull this trash off him." The moment he's through the door, my fist is up and ready for contact, but someone grabs me and a fist slams into the side of my face. Two arms grip me, holding my hands behind my back. Mack pushes himself off the ground and stands in front of me.

"You fucking bastard." He punches me, once, twice in the face and a third time in the gut. "You will make sure Skylar returns home with me. I don't give a fuck how you end it with her, but I will go home with my family. Either you take me up on my end and she goes willingly, or we do it my way, a not-so-willing way. Make the right choice. For her. Do you hear me?"

I'm breathing hard, and with each breath my chest feels like it's going to explode.

"Hey!" Conner yells, sprinting through the door and standing between me and Mack. "Get the fuck out of here!" he yells. The man behind me lets go, and he and his boss walk away. I hear the faint sound of a laugh before he closes the driver's door to a black Lincoln Town Car. Conner grabs my wrist before I can take another step.

"What in the hell was that?" he asks.

"Nothing," I answer, coughing.

"That was definitely not nothing," he says, pointing to the spot where Mack's car just disappeared from.

I fucking know that, but what can I tell him? I don't know what he wants me to say. Clearly, I don't know as much as I should about Sky's past, and it doesn't even matter. She's in danger with that guy sticking around. *This shit doesn't happen in real life.* The girl I'm seeing was engaged to that guy. Truth or not, there's no fucking way I can let her leave with him. I don't want to imagine how he treats her.

But, if I don't give him what he wants, how much danger is she still in?

"Luke," Conner hollers at me as I head inside.

There is no way I'm sharing any of this with anyone.

"He was just some drunk who got out of control."

"I didn't see you serve him."

"He was drunk when he showed up. I refused to serve him and tried to get him to leave."

Conner takes in my appearance. I keep walking; I don't

need him getting a good look and starting back up with questions. I can't have him worrying to the point he says something to Alexis, who will tell Sky. I should probably make sure Beth knows it was nothing too. Just another random drunk at the bar.

"Man makes a real mean drunk. I think you made the right choice. The whole jumping over the bar thing though? You could have walked around. I mean it was cool as shit, but wow."

He laughs, and I force myself to join him.

"Go clean yourself up. Can't make money with a bloody face."

He pats my shoulder as he passes me. He's ready to get back to work, but all I can think about is everything that just happened. Do I call the cops? Do I ask Sky about it? Tell my mom and sisters to never leave their house again?

I don't want to make the wrong choice, but how am I going to know what's the right decision for a situation like this?

I don't think there is one.

Skylar

I'm turning into such a sap. I know this because I'm sitting on the couch down in the store, waiting for Luke to get off work. He said he was going to come by tonight, but being upstairs was driving me crazy. I've already cleaned everything I can, and there isn't much for me to down here either. I just want to keep busy. Clearly, I still get nervous when I'm going to see Luke. Not in a nervous scared way but in a nervous excited I-can't-wait-to-kiss-him way. Luke's shadow passes by the front window, and I jump up, making my way to greet him at the door.

I'm positive that if there were people across the street, they would have heard the gasp I just let out.

"What happened to your eye?"

I reach up to touch it, but he flinches away.

"There was a misunderstanding with a box on the top shelf in storage room," he answers quickly. Almost too quickly. My head tilts as I look him in the eyes. Come to think of it, his tone just now reminds me of the day Sara gave me a job at the bar. That day, he was doing something kind for his mother.

"The box just fell?"

"I'm fine, really."

"Did it bounce from your eye to your jaw? Is that how you got that bruise, too?" I ask, turning his face to get a better look.

He sighs and leans against the wall. His eyes take on a glossy appearance as they look into mine.

"Luke, what's wrong?"

"I …" He focuses on the shelf behind me. "I …"

"Luke," I step back. His shaky voice is making my heart race. "What is it? You're starting to scare me."

Another sigh and then his hands tug on his hair as he groans loudly and grabs my hand.

"Some guy got too drunk tonight and things got physical."

"I'll say." Finally, the truth. "Why wouldn't you just tell me that?"

"I don't want you to worry about going to work or anything."

"I think dealing with drunk people is sort of a given when

you work in a bar, Luke." I roll my eyes at him and head for the apartment.

"You are too good to me, you know that?"

I stop.

"I have my days, but then again, so do you," I say, taking a step toward him since he's only made it as far at the front counter.

"I just want you to know how much you mean to me. I should show it more."

"Luke." I wrap my arms around him and squeeze. Luke leans down to kiss me, and when his tongue passes my lips, he grips the back of my legs and lifts me to the counter.

I lock my ankles behind his back and tighten my grip, pressing myself against his groin. I pull my lips away from him to kiss his cheek, his jawline. He returns the same motions, moving down between my breasts. With my arms around his waist, I tug and he flinches.

"Where all did he hit you?"

"It's fine," he says and then kisses me again, trying to distract me from more questions. It works, too.

A moan escapes me as Luke grinds his hips into mine. Then he takes a step back and switches his view to the front window. Stepping away from me, he quickly closes the blinds.

I can't help but smile. "Good idea. Wouldn't want to make anyone jealous."

He laughs at my remark, right before capturing my lips in a kiss once again. He takes a nip at my bottom lip, hooking his fingers over my shorts to pull them down. He pauses. "Why aren't you wearing any panties?"

I give him a wicked grin.

He crashes his lips back to mine and jerks me against his

groin. Desperate fingers grip the bottom of my shirt, pulling it over my head and tossing it to the floor. We should probably move this upstairs, but this is one of the best parts of Luke. He's impulsive, and I crave it.

"What kind of buckle is this?" I break our kiss to look down at his belt buckle, only that isn't what is on display at this moment. Instead of answering me, he unclips the belt and whips it off. After that, I don't lose any time pulling his jeans down.

"Let's try a new position," I say when he's pulled the condom from his jean pocket. He rips it open, covering himself.

"I have a feeling you have an idea already," he says.

Slowly, I nudge him back with my foot and slide off the counter. I turn and bend, my backside bare in front of him.

I breathe in deeply as he takes a step forward. My hair flips down my back as I peek over my shoulder. His eyes are raking over my body.

"Is this okay?"

He runs a hand down my back until his palm reaches the spot where I crave his touch most. He leans over me, his cheek against mine.

"Everything with you is more than okay, Sky."

My head drops to the counter as he positions himself behind me. With an easy thrust of his hips, he enters me slowly. My breathing picks up, as does his with each motion. The moment I press to the tips of my toes, he sinks deeper, losing all control. He grips my hips and pulls me back against him with each thrust. It sounds wrong, the noises our bodies make when they slap against each other, but the whimpers coming from him and from me—that's how I know every-thing about this is right.

"Luke," I practically purr.

He pulls out fast, flipping me over, propping me back on the counter, and entering me before I can protest.

"Oh!" I pant as he slams into me.

"Sky." He picks up the pace. I cover his lips with my own, clashing our tongues as I reach around to grip his ass. My orgasm rips through my body.

"Luke!"

His primal grunt when my head drops back is a sure sign what's happening to me is happening to him, too.

Smiling at each other like fools, we put our clothes back in place.

"Come on," he says, lacing our fingers together. "Let's get to bed." He leads me up the stairs with purpose, but I don't miss the fact he looks back, past me, twice. My gut tells me something more happened tonight and he doesn't want to share. I won't force him to tell me everything, but he should want to, right?

CHAPTER TWENTY

Skylar

Luke opened the store for the first time in months today, and we are working the first shift together. He was able to get his close friends, Conner, Logan, and Ethan in here over the course of a few days, and they moved all the shelves. They ended up rearranging an entire row to line the back wall to make more room. I like it. It makes the space look larger, and even though Luke won't admit it, I know he likes the layout better now, too.

I close the door behind me, a chill running over my body from the snowy breeze that showed up early this morning. Luke should be here soon with lunch. Shoveling a small walking path for him is the least I can do since he went out in this freezing weather. I plug in the Christmas lights we hung around the front windows and tug my crimson sweater tighter around my body as I walk to the back of the store to find a small heater I can use under the front counter. Heat sounds like a fantastic idea while I check in new inventory.

The bell rings over the door just as I am about to open up a new box of books. I let the cardboard lid flop close and peek around the end of the row. I have a smile on, ready to greet another customer, when my eyes register the man standing the doorway.

This is not happening. This can't be happening. I'm imagining this again.

My hands are shaking and my heart is racing. Where is my new phone? It was an early Christmas gift from everyone at the bar. I didn't have much choice other than to accept it, but I'm glad I have it at this moment. I want to call or text Luke and tell him he needs to get back here, now.

"Skylar, we need to talk." Mack strides down the aisle. His dark hair is buzzed short like normal, and his blue eyes are still bright. His smile is one I've seen a million times, and I swallow back the tears. My ex-fiancé arriving out of the blue isn't a good sign. Of everyone I ever thought would look for me, Mack didn't come to mind even once. Nothing I did was ever good enough for him. What reason could he possibly have to be here now? To tell me I'm disappointing him or making him look like a fool again?

I cross my arms and look away. I can't look at him.

"Mack, I don't know why you're here, but—"

"But you missed me as much as I missed you?" He cuts me off in a sweet tone that I've never, *ever* heard from him before. He takes another step forward and I take another back.

"I don't have anything to say to you, and I think you should leave." I step around him, heading for the front counter where I remember leaving my phone. He follows. The moment I grab my cell, he places his hand over mine, stalling me from reaching out to Luke.

"Don't call him, Skylar. He isn't the guy you think he is. I'm the one you need, and looking at this place"—he glances around—"you do need me."

Don't call him, Skylar. He isn't the guy you think he is.

How does he know about Luke? Unless …

"You've been watching me!" I shout. His head jerks back, probably not expecting such a vocal reaction. He's used to a girl who did everything she was told. I'm not that girl anymore. I'm a woman who knows what she wants and who is motivated to get it. A woman who defends herself. Who requires respect from everyone she meets no matter their financial status. I'm not a puppet for anyone, not anymore.

"Skylar, ladies don't have outburst like—"

"Do not come in here and wave your hand at me as if I need to stop talking, Mack." I yank my hand out from under his and step around the counter. "I knew I saw your car the other night. How long have you been following me?"

He sighs. His brows dip together as he flicks his gray suit jacket back to rest his hands on his sides. His head drops for a brief moment before he looks at me. "Only since your boyfriend called me and your father threatening your life unless we paid a rather large sum."

I swallow and my hand lands on my chest as I take a deep breath. Luke needs money, but he would never do something that extreme. *Would he?*

"You can't blame yourself, Skylar. I sent Clayton, my most trusted right-hand man, down here, and from what he's told me, it looks like you've been fooled thoroughly."

"I don't believe you," I say, fighting back my urge to cry. My phone is still in my hand; I type out a quick text telling

Luke there is an emergency at the store, so he needs to get here quickly.

"He may not have been planning to ever hurt you, but he definitely is using you for money. Skylar, this is why people like him and people like us don't mix. His kind of people don't know how to earn and create success. They are desperate and will do anything they can to have money handed to them. Luke is no different."

Mack takes a step toward me. I shake my head, and he stops.

Luke wouldn't. He said it wasn't like that.

The first tear falls over my cheek.

"Come home with me. Let me take care of you the way we planned before you left."

Even if Luke confirms everything Mack just said, there is no way I'll ever go back with my ex. He is part of the life and lies I ran from in the first place. I wipe the tear away, and when I have Mack's attention, I say, "I'm sorry if I hurt you when I left, but nothing has changed. I don't want that life. I want my own life where I'm in charge."

I see the tick in his jaw as he grinds his teeth. "You don't know what you want."

He must be hard of hearing.

"I just told you—"

"You're confused. I just gave you upsetting information, so you're thinking rashly and saying things you don't really mean."

"I'm not a child, Mack."

"No, you're—"

"Sky!" Luke rushes through the door so quickly it bounces off the wall behind, rattling the window. His shoulders drop when he sees me, then he engulfs me in a hug. His shirt is damp. He must have run here. "I thought something happened to you." He steps back, his eyes surveying every inch of me.

"What did you—" He cuts himself off when he notices Mack. I'm expecting him to be confused, but he isn't; the look in his eyes tells me he recognizes my ex-fiancé.

Oh my god. Mack was right.

It does surprise me though when Luke nudges me behind him as he stands between me and Mack.

"Leave," Luke says in a voice more intimidating than my own father's used to be.

"I don't think so. Not without Skylar," Mack replies, his chest puffing out as he stands tall. Luke is a good foot and half taller than Mack. Both are in great shape, but I know without a doubt that Luke would win if anyone were to start throwing punches.

"Actually, you're going to walk through that door right now before I knock you out and have to drag you. And before I have you thrown in jail for stalking Skylar and threating her life," Luke threatens.

"What?" My eyes flash between Luke and Mack.

"He came to the BA to—"

"To tell him that I refuse to let him use my fiancé against me," Mack whines, completely out of character and cutting Luke off before he can finish.

"What, no!" Luke hollers.

"You really called Mack asking for money or you'd hurt me?" I ask.

"That's absurd, Sky. Is that what he told you?" Worried eyes filled with hope land on mine.

"Well, you did need money for this place," I answer. What if he was willing to go a step too far to get what he wanted?

"Nothing is more important than you. I swear it on my life, on my mother's life, and everyone else we know. I never called him or anyone for money. I told you that you could trust me, and I meant every word."

Maybe he—

"Don't let him lie to you, Skylar. Fooling others is clearly something he's good at." Mack cuts in, stepping closer to Luke.

"I'm not lying, Sky. You have to believe me. I would give up everything I have to be with you." Luke's hand finds mine as his voice grows soft. He rubs his thumb over mine. My eyes lock with his as he says, "I—"

"Oh, what a crock of—"

Mack doesn't get to finish his sentence before Luke right hooks him across the face. I press my lips together, hiding my smile. I have no idea what's really going on, but I don't feel bad for Mack.

"Mack, you need to go," I say, heading for the door and holding it open for him.

"You can't be serious." He spits out as he wipes a small bit of blood from his mouth. He moves toward me.

"Touch her, and I'll smash more than just your face." Luke warns.

Mack stops just in the doorway. A darkness sets in his eyes that sends a shiver from my head to my toes.

"I won't leave without you. You'll figure it out, Skylar. I know you will. You'll make the right choice," he says before storming out.

He keeps his focus on me as he walks by the window. I

know that look. I used to see it every day when he was close to closing a deal at the office. It means he won't give up till he has what he wants.

Luke

My fingers clench the hair on my head as I whip around to face her.

"I don't know what's happening, but I never called him for money. He came into the BA and told me that I need to stay away from you. Said if I broke your heart, he would write me a check. If I didn't do it, he'd find another way to take you back with him."

"Were you going to?"

"No, I didn't even consider it."

"So you honestly never once thought you could use me for money?"

"Not before. Not now. Not ever, Sky."

This wouldn't be happening if I had just told her.

"All you talk about is how you can make things better for your mom and your sisters. I know you think that if you had more money, it would all be easier. I just don't know how far you're willing to go to make that happen."

"Sky, we can't keep fighting about this. You either believe me or you don't."

"I've been used my whole life, Luke; I don't want that to be the case with you, too."

"It's not. I swear it, please don't believe him. I would trade this place for you with no second thoughts or regrets."

"So it's probably safe to say that drunk guy at the bar the other night was actually Mack."

I nod.

"You should have just told me."

"Like you told me you used to be engaged."

Weary eyes watch me, studying me until her shoulders drop with the breath she lets go.

"Why can't we just … be honest with each other?"

"We come from different lives is all. Learning to make one together isn't going to be easy, but if we want it, we keep trying. Right?"

"Right."

I kiss the top of her head and then rest my cheek there. "We need to call the police or someone, Sky. That guy wants trouble, and I don't think he's leaving here without causing some."

"He'll leave. He won't waste his time on something he can't control."

"I'm not sure about that. I think he's planning to control this situation."

"Luke, I grew up with Mack. He'd never do something that would tarnish his company's reputation."

"I honestly believe that—"

"Luke, I don't want to argue with you."

"But I think something needs to be done, or he'll be back."

"He won't be back."

"You're so sure about it?" I ask.

"Yes."

"Fine." My gut tells me the guy isn't leaving. If Sky won't believe me enough to be cautious, I'll just have to make sure I'm around to protect her. "Let's close up and head upstairs."

"I think you should stay at your place tonight," she says without looking at me.

If Mack comes back tonight, she'll be alone. I take a huge breath and release the fists my hands have formed.

"Yeah, okay."

In one big step I'm in front of her, pulling her toward me and crashing my mouth onto hers. The sweet taste of lemon meets my lips. I press harder, her tongue sliding its way into my mouth. She's kissing me back. That's a good sign. But it's not enough for her to want me to stay. I don't look back as I walk out of the store. How do I make her see that I just want her to be safe?

CHAPTER TWENTY-ONE

Skylar

Dinner is cooked and ready to go for the moment Luke arrives. It wasn't on my list, but I've always wanted to cook a meal for someone else. I hope I did okay. Both Alex and Beth said you can't mess up spaghetti.

They had better be right.

I put the cheesy toast into the oven and set the timer for six minutes.

Six minutes and Luke will be here. *Thankfully.*

It was silly of me to doubt him for even a second last night after Mack showed up. He looked so scared when he thought I wasn't going to believe him. I don't know how, but I saw myself in that look and because I hadn't done what I'd been accused of doing, I knew he didn't try to get money from my father either. I don't understand why we keep doubting each other. Am I insecure? Is he? It doesn't matter. I want this to work.

The rattle of knuckles on the door startles me into a slight jump. I twist, facing the entrance and immediately know the rapping isn't Luke. Luke just walks in, and the girls knock once before entering.

The knocking resumes, this time louder. By the time I reach the door, I really, *really* wish there was a little peephole to look through, but why do I need one when you have to get through the bookstore to get up here? And the bookstore was locked last time I checked.

"Open the door, Skylar. I know you're home." Mack's voice flows through the door, sending spikes of fear all over my body. I step back and don't answer the door.

"Go home, Mack. I don't know why you're still here."

"Just let me in so we can talk about it."

"Mack, just go. There isn't anything to talk about. I'm sorry."

"You're going to open this door, Skylar." There is a warning in his voice. "We're going to talk this out, face to face, whether I have to break this fucking door down or you open it like the fucking lady your mother taught you to be."

He can't see me, but that doesn't stop the tears from starting or me from shaking my head no.

"Skylar."

I don't say anything. My eyes flash around the room looking for something, anything I can defend myself with. *Where is that damn phone?*

"Skylar," his voice is lower now and angrier. "Open. The. Door."

I still don't make a sound as I back into the kitchen.

"Skylar!" he yells one last time before he breaks the lock and the door flies open to bounce off the wall behind it. Mack steps in, looking the part of a man who hasn't slept in nights, but with determination in his eyes. He isn't leaving here until he gets what he came for.

A scream slips past my lips. I turn, sprinting for the drawer with my kitchen knives, but Mack is faster than I am. His arms wrap around me. A hand grips my wrist and twists it till the knife drops from my fingers. I cry out as a burning pain darts up my arms. He shoves me to the ground and stands above me.

Cradling the arm he injured, I scoot back against the wall. I watch him as he surveys the room, his neck turning slowly. I catch the tick in his jaw when his eyes fall on the table.

"A fucking candlelight dinner for two, huh? I never got that sort of treatment. Why not? I gave you everything."

"Mack, things are different now. You deserve someone who will give you this, but that woman isn't me."

Two fists come down on the table, causing the plates, silverware, and everything else to bounce into a new position. "I don't fucking want anyone else!"

"Mack."

A wicked laugh comes from deep inside him as he watches me. "You can't use your sweet voice to change my mind. You're my fiancée, and I'm not leaving here without you." He jerks me back up to my feet and shoves me forward. My hip hits the table. I catch a view of the dinner knifes on the table. I didn't need them for spaghetti, but I'm relieved more than ever that I still put them out. I don't think twice as I reach for the knife and swing at him. I don't know what I'm doing. My eyes close as I swing again and again, until I hear him cry out. Opening one eye, I see I've struck his arm and now he's lunging for me. My back hits the table, knocking it over, and the fire from the candle catches on the cloth. A blaze begins on the floor of the apartment. I kick back at him to get him off me as I crawl on the floor toward the sink. I have to get water on the fire before it's too late. Except I don't reach the sink. Something hits my head from behind. Everything goes blurry and then black.

* * *

My eyes hurt to open, and I can't stop coughing. The room is filled with a haze, and I can't see anything. I cough more, pushing myself to my knees to stand. The smile on Mack's face comes into view. "If you're not going to be with me, you won't be with anyone, Skylar."

Pain consumes me the moment he strikes my face. I stumble but manage to crawl away from him. I can't see anything, so instead I feel around until I'm on the other side of my bed, the same side that is near the apartment door.

"You can't run from me. Every time you make a noise, I will find you."

I hold my breath, my hands touching every inch of the wall behind me as I try to place exactly where I am and how many steps I might have to the door. It will bring attention to me the moment I open it and the smoke starts to rush out, but it's hot in here, and if I don't get out fast I'm not sure I ever will.

I can't hold it any longer. My coughing resumes, and I take two quick steps for the door before a hand clenches around my throat. My fists beat and punch at his chest, but it's not working. He isn't losing his grip. My fingers curl as I dig my nails into the skin around his wrists. Still, his hold on me is tight. The smoke burns my eyes, and I close them, praying I'll be able to open them again soon and this will all be over.

Luke

I tossed and turned all night, dreaming of Sky alone in that apartment. I had nightmares that Mack showed up and she left with him. I hate when dreams feel like real life. So when she texted me this morning, inviting me over for dinner. I packed a bag of clothes before I left, praying she'd let me stay the night at her place.

I'm about a block from the store when the smell of smoke creeps in through my rolled down window. I look around me but don't see where it's coming from.

I turn the corner and see a few people gathered around the store. Smoke coming from the roof. I slam on the brakes and the car skids from the ice on the road. I manage to stop the car, jam the gear into park, and take off with the best ice-restricted sprint I can.

"Sky!" I shout, searching faces in the crowd. "Sky!"

Wide-eyed faces stare back at me as I keep yelling. I don't see her.

"I saw a man go in there not too long ago. I don't think he ever came out," a woman to my right says to another woman. My heart drops into my stomach and then lurches up to my throat as I take off for the entrance. *That bastard!*

"You can't go in there!" a man voice roars behind me when I reach the front door.

"This is my store!" I yell back. "Call 911!"

"The building is on fire, son. It's not safe for you to go in there!"

I can see it's on fucking fire.

"My girlfriend, she lives in the apartment upstairs!" I scream back and take that moment to go inside. I have to make sure she's not in there.

The store is filled with smoke and it's warm, but the flames haven't made their way down here yet. Waving smoke away from my face, I reach the bottom of the stairwell in record time. I take the steps two at a time until I reach the top. Her door is open and a glow of fire can be through the entire place.

"Sky!" I call out.

Nothing.

"Sky!"

Nothing.

"Skylar!" I give it my best this time.

"She wasn't supposed to pick you." I hear him, but I can't see him. "She was supposed to pick me," he says again, and I move toward his voice. "Now, *now* she won't be able to pick either of us."

Fingers grip my ankle, jerking me back. I fall forward, my hand reaching out to stop myself from hitting the ground. Only it doesn't hit the ground without touching flesh first. When I'm able to push myself up, all I make out in the haze is an unconscious Sky. I pull her to me and get to my feet. With her slumped over my shoulder, I head back for the door. Again, a hand grabs my ankle, but this time I balance myself to kick. I hit him right in the face and leave him lying on the floor. When his grip loosens, I dash down the steps with Sky and out the door. People cheer as I bring her out and lay her on the ground. She coughs, giving me hope that she is okay. A woman rushes to help her as I look back up at the burning apartment.

I'm a fucking idiot.

I make it back up the stairs and hook an arm around Mack to help him out. He's barely conscious and leans most of his weight on me. His feet are dragging by the time we make it to the street, and I can hear the sirens close by. I don't lay him down near as gently as I did Sky. I actually find joy when his head bounces a little.

Sky is where I left her; the lady is now on her phone providing details of what happened. Even with all the soot covering her face, it's obvious Sky is injured badly. The urge the beat Mack while he's unconscious or to put him back inside the building is strong. The need to make sure Sky is safe is stronger.

I strip off my coat and my shirt. I wrap her leg with my shirt and then cover her with my coat as I hold her in my arms. Her eyes flutter over and over as she continues to look up at me. Her lips are moving, but she isn't actually saying anything and then she coughs and it sounds like it's coming from somewhere deep. She coughs and winces a couple more times before settling back into my arms.

The people who are standing all around us are on their phones. Someone must have called it in because a fire truck is pulling up.

"Luke." It comes out in a whisper, but one word is all she has to say to keep my full attention.

"I'm here. Don't worry, I'm here."

"I'm so sorry," she whispers again. Her eyes have stopped fluttering and she looks more responsive now.

"You didn't do anything wrong, Sky. No need to apologize."

"But the apartment is gone."

"And you're alive—that's all that matters."

An ambulance pulls up on the curb in front of us and two EMTs rush out.

"How long was she in there?"

"What caused the fire?"

"I … I…" I can't find the words because I don't know the answers.

"Sir, please give us room," one of them says to me, pushing me out of the way. I don't want to let her go. "Sir, please, you will have to step back."

I do as they ask because I don't want to stop them from helping Sky, but it feels like a hook, piercing my heart over and over in the same wounded spot.

I watch as they lift her on to the orange board. Watch as they stick a needle in her arm and strap her down. Watch as they lift her into the truck. The doors start to close when I grip on to the handle, ready to jump in to ride with her.

"Sir, are you family?"

"I'm her boyfriend." My answer is hurried.

"I'm sorry, sir, you'll have to meet us at Summit Hospital. You can't ride in here unless your immediate family."

"She needs me!" I refuse to take no for an answer.

"Sir, please step down. She needs to get to an emergency room."

I don't argue this time because I just want her to be okay. I *need* her to be okay. Someone says my name, but I ignore them. I'm focused on Sky, and the last thing I see before they close the doors is her eyes on me.

CHAPTER TWENTY-TWO

Luke

I've hated hospital rooms ever since I sat in one waiting to hear whether or not I was going to ever be able to speak to my father again. Maybe my hatred comes from the fact the outcome then was that I'd never get to speak or hug or do anything with him for the rest of my life.

"She's going to be fine, man," Conner assures me for the hundredth time. I know Sky was talking to me after I pulled her out of the store, but that doesn't mean something couldn't have had an aftereffect. It was clear she has a bruise across her face, a broken leg, and three broken fingers. She was in a fire. She could have burns I didn't notice. And that was just the outside. I don't even want to think about her lungs or her brain. What if she hit her head wrong, or her lungs are failing from the smoke? Mack did a number on her. If he weren't in a hospital room himself being watched around the clock by the local police, I'd be out looking for that sorry son of a bitch and leaving him with ten times worse than what did to Sky.

"I keep thinking I should have stayed with her. I knew that guy was watching her. I just … I didn't think—"

"There was no way for you to know that he would do something like this."

"The fact I even knew he was in town should have raised a red flag, and in a way it did. I just didn't think he would try to kill her. I didn't think people like that actually existed. Thought it was all in big cities and the movies."

"Desperate people do desperate things. You can't blame yourself."

But I do.

I glance up at the clock. It's been six hours. Someone should have come out by now. I start to pace the room, looking out the small window of the door. The same clerk who was here when we arrived is still sitting behind the desk. She must know I'm looking at her because she spots me. Her eyes narrow. I may have made a bit of a scene when they wouldn't answer my questions after the first hour. I'm not family. What kind of bullshit is that? I am her family. Her friends are her family.

The nurse's view of me is blocked by a fancy charcoal suit and a shimmering red dress that's accompanied by more diamonds than I've ever seen in my life. The nurse points toward the door I'm peering through, and the couple looks at me. I meet the woman's eyes first. Although they are red rimmed, they look exactly like Sky's.

I can't believe her parents are here.

Now they're moving in my direction.

"Fuck," I shout, causing everyone in the room—Conner, Alex, Beth, and Sarah—to jump in their seats. "Sky's parents are here."

"I thought they disowned her." Alex stands.

"They're probably coming to cover up whatever attention this is going to put on them. Sky hasn't told me much, but they don't sound like very good people."

The next thing I know, the door is opening and her parents are standing in front of me. Sky has been through too much tonight to have to put up with this bullshit, too. I'll use them to get as much information as I can out of the nurse, and then I'll make sure they get the message to leave. Sky is happy without them.

"You must be Luke." Her father offers his hand to me. I take it and give him the firmest shake I can.

"Should I know you?" I ask.

He smiles, but it's not a real smile. It looks exactly like the smile Sky used to have before … well, before I fell in love with her.

"I wouldn't imagine you would and if you had, I'm certain it wouldn't have been anything positive. My name is Maxwell Atwood, Skylar's father."

"Clayton called us," her mother says from behind him. Her voice soft, just like Sky's. For a family that's so much alike on the outside, how can they be so different on the inside?

"I'm sorry. I don't know who that is."

"I'm Skylar's mother," she adds. "Clayton is Mack's cousin. He called us earlier this evening. Told us Mack was trying to bring Skylar home, but that he had a bad feeling something was going to happen. Something that might hurt our daughter."

"We tried to reach her," her father adds, "but her line has been disconnected."

"She's been living here for *months,* and tonight was the night you just learned that her phone line was disconnected?" My voice is rising, but I don't care. No parents should treat their child the way these two have. "Did you not care she was living in the park or that she went nights without food?"

"Luke." Beth's hand rests over my forearm.

"Or that all she wanted in life was to make her own decisions, paint her fucking fingernails pink, and own a dog!" I shrug Beth's off arm. I don't want to be touched right now.

"Luke," Conner says my name this time.

"All she wanted was to be herself, and you controlled her. You were actually going to force her to marry someone of your choice and not hers. I just can't—"

"Luke." Three of them shout my name this time and I finally stop. Sky's mother is in tears, and her father looks guilty. It's only when someone nudges my arm that I notice the doctor standing in the doorway.

"Are you Skylar's family?" he asks. I step forward before anyone else has the chance.

"Yes, I am," I answer immediately.

The doctor's uneasy eyes glance around the room. He stops on Skylar's father, who makes the best choice he can around me right now and nods his head.

"She's in recovery. The smoke caused some problems with her breathing, but she is hooked up to a machine that is helping her breathe easier. No long-term problems. She has three broken fingers in her right hand, two fractured ribs, we moved her left shoulder back in place, and were able to stitch up her few gashes. Her left leg was broken in two spots. Surgery went well, but she is on a lot of painkillers. It's going to take her some time to heal; she'll need someone to assist with her normal day-to-day activities when she is released. She's pretty banged up, but she is lucky there are no internal injuries."

"Can I see her?" I ask. He said she's going to be fine, but until I see her, I won't be.

"She's sleeping, but it would be okay for one of you to go in." This time he looks to her mother. "Ma'am?"

My mouth is halfway open to protest when her father says, "I think Luke should be the one who is there when she wakes up."

My mind won't be easily swayed about these two, but I am thankful that they clearly recognize their mistakes and, for once, made a choice for their daughter that she would support.

I follow behind the doctor, ignoring the glare from the nurse's station. We ride the elevator up two floors, and when the door opens the doctor says, "She came off the anesthesia about an hour ago, so feel free to talk to her while she sleeps. You can hold her hand, but be gentle with her."

I want to growl out that I'm not an idiot. But he's just doing his job. If I had been doing mine, we wouldn't even be here right now.

Skylar's is at the end of the hall. Once the doctor leaves, I stand outside for a moment.

My heart hurts. Every piece of my body hurts. I didn't handle my father's death well, but I dealt with it. I stayed strong and I kept myself together. With Sky, the moment they took her away from me in that ambulance, I swear my heart stopped. I cried on the drive here, although no one knows that. I wouldn't give a crap if they did. My chest felt like it was going to crumble to pieces right there on the car floor.

That was the moment I knew that life without Sky isn't a

life I want. Ever. Who cares if she's been here for only a few months and who cares that part of that time we never spoke, another part we butted heads, and the shortest part of all was when we became an *us*? All that matters is that she is alive and she is safe.

After listening to Mack claim her like she was his property, it got me thinking. Yes, I want her to end up with me, but most of all I want her to want that and choose me. Choose to be happy and to be herself. If she wants all those things without me, I'll let her go. But god, please let her pick me.

With the twist of the knob, I take a deep breath and step inside her room. My breath catches when I see her. She's awake and she's beautiful.

Skylar

Waking up to an empty room breaks my heart. I was awake in the ambulance so I knew I would end up here, although it does take me a minute or two to remember everything. Once I do, the tears are uncontrollable. Luke isn't here, and I don't know where he went. He was holding my hand when the ambulance arrived, and the last thing I saw before they closed the ambulance doors was a police officer approaching him.

When the hospital room door opens and I see his face, I don't care that I can see only out of one eye or that the left side of my body feels like a semi-truck ran me over. All I care about is that he's here. He's safe.

He pauses in the doorway, and my vision glazes over when I see him wipe away at his own tear. He swallows and then rushes to me. I can see his struggle to figure out how to comfort me without hurting me because he reaches out to touch me but stops. He settles for sitting next to my bed and holding my hand.

"I can't believe that bastard tried to kill you."

"I'm sorry about the bookstore," I say, wishing for once since I left home that I had the money to give to him. He needs it more than ever after the fire.

"Seriously." He pulls back and kisses my forehead. "You could have died, and the first thing you have to say is about the store?" He laughs.

"I know how much it means to you and how hard you worked to make it the business it was. I wasn't the person who broke in the first two times, but I am to blame for it being on fire."

"No, don't even think that. Mack is the one who's at fault. Not you."

"Had I never shown up in Wind Valley, he never would have either."

"The guy is mental no matter where you are, Sky."

"I know, but—" I stop myself. "I don't want to be responsible for anything else ruining your life. If I just go home, back to Seattle, then I can—"

"Move back? Why would you do that?" He jerks back as if someone had slapped him.

"If I move back, the trouble I seem to have following me can't be brought onto you and your family. A lot more people could have been hurt, Luke. What if it were you, or your mom, or even your sister? I could never forgive myself for that."

"I don't care about all that. I mean, I do, but none of it matters without you."

"We've only been dating a few months, and even though I've fallen in love with you, that's exactly why I have to do this," I tell him.

"You love me?"

"More than you'll ever know," I say. *Great, here come more tears.*

"Sky, if you love me anything like I love you, you can't leave now."

And tears.

"I'm so sorry, Luke. I have to."

Luke turns, looking away from me. His head drops. "Is that really what you want?"

No.

"It's the right choice."

"But is it what you want?" he repeats.

"What I want and what I need to do to keep you safe are two different things, Luke."

"I'm not safe if I don't have you," he says.

"Don't say that."

"It's the truth. I've never been so scared in my entire life than in that moment when I thought I would lose you forever. You came here to find out who you are and to do what you want—don't let go of that. Mack is going to jail for a really long time, Sky. Shit, his cousin helped him find you and then called your parents to tell on him when he thought you were in danger. The only trouble that follows you is no longer a threat, Sky. Don't leave because you think it's best; leave only if that is what you really want." He kneels next to my bed, still holding my hand.

"I love you, Sky, and if what you *really* want is to be here with me, I want that more than anything else in this entire world."

How do I still have tears left to cry?

"I want to stay with you," I whisper. He leans down to kiss me but changes his mind when he spots the gash on my lip. I don't need a mirror to know it's there. I feel like there is golf ball stuck to my face. He places a kiss on my forehead instead.

"I'm sure Eloise and Maxwell Atwood were too busy to hear the news," I say, jumping back to his mention of my parents. I'm sure the message went right to my father's assistant and that was it. It's probably still in a pile of unread messages.

"Well"—Luke's face mashes up with too many expressions for me to decide if what he's about to say is good or bad —"your parents may or may not be in the waiting room, and I may or may not have made the best impression on your dad. Not that I think I matters, but yeah."

"My parents are here?"

My heart starts to race, and for the first time since I woke, I wish I had more painkillers.

"Yeah, do you want to talk to them?"

"No," I answer quickly. "I mean, yes, but not right now."

I need to figure out how I feel about this first. They came here? For me? They've never shown concern for me before, and now they've flown to another state. Is it because they thought I was going to die? Or do they actually care? Maybe even miss me ...

"Okay, well, can I get you anything?" Luke asks, pulling up the chair to sit right next to the bed and lacing his fingers with mine.

"Just talk to me about nothing and everything until I fall asleep," I tell him, and he does. I think he talks for a full three minutes before everything goes black.

* * *

I think I'm going to be sick.

I told Luke after I woke up the second time that I was ready to see my parents. Which was a total lie, but considering they most likely won't leave until they get to speak to me, I figure I better just get it over with. Now I'm just sitting in my room, alone, since Beth left. Something is going on with her. I know this is an emotional situation, but she cried, too. Of all the friends I've made here, Beth is the most stable. Then she said she was late for something and rushed out of here.

"Sky, are you ready?" Luke asks, holding the door open so I can see only him.

I nod.

Luke steps to the side as my parents enter the room. It's obvious my father is upset. I can't remember if his hair was this white when I left. It's only been a few months.

My mother is playing the devastated mother role beautifully. She's crying, loudly I might add.

"Oh, Skylar, I was worried about you," she sobs. She doesn't even step close to the bed or check to make sure her daughter is in one piece. Nope, not my mom. She dabs at the fake tears with a Kleenex. Then she looks at my father, like "okay, I've done my part."

I follow her gaze and have no idea how to process what I'm looking at.

My father hasn't moved as he stands at the end of my bed. Luke walks around him to stand opposite my mother. He sits, grabbing my hand as he does so.

The moment I see my father's chest begin to shake, I know I can't look at him. Maxwell Atwood has never shed a tear in my whole life. Not one time can I remember him being upset over anything. If I look at him now though, I'll know it was me. That I broke him down. That my life was in danger enough to finally show me the kind of father I always wanted.

I look to Luke, who isn't watching me. He's watching my dad.

"Skylar," my dad's voice grabs my attention. "I'm sorry, so, so sorry."

He drops to sit on the end of my bed. "I didn't know." His lip is shaking. "I've never wanted for anything. I was handed the company when my father passed. I never thought twice about any of it." He finds my uninjured leg and squeezes my ankle. "I thought if it was everything I ever needed, it would be good enough for my daughter."

"It was good enough—it just isn't the life I want."

He nods slowly.

Was this his plan? To come in here and immediately go into everything we haven't said but should have said a long time ago? My mother is the same old person she always has been, but my father, he's changed. And I don't have to question it. I can see it. He is nothing like the father I left. I left a man who didn't care enough to apologize or to cry or listen to me when I spoke. The man in front of me is doing all those things.

"Perhaps I should have asked you or paid more attention to the woman you have become. Maybe I would have noticed that you are nothing like I was at that age. And Mack"—he chokes up, his hand covers his heart—"I had no idea. When I called his father to tell him what happened, he had the balls to reveal he knew something wasn't right when Mack stopped taking his medication the week you left. His *medication*." Dad stands, paces for a moment before leaning on the wall near the door. "How did I miss that? How could I have overlooked something so huge?"

"Maxwell, if we want to make the jet's flight time, we had better go," my mother says.

"Sit down," he snaps. "You almost lost your daughter and your concern right now is to make a flight on time? Either you sit there and be quiet, you actually help your daughter, or you leave. I don't care what you choose. It's time we put Skylar first."

I don't cry when she gets up and walks out. Neither does my father.

"I'm sorry about your mother." He shakes his head.

"Don't be. She's the same old mother I've always known."

"I'll be in town for a few days, as long as you need me and until you are ready to come home."

"Actually, Dad, I'm going to stay here."

"In Wyoming?"

"Yes."

"With this young man, I assume?"

We both look at Luke, whose eyes are wide with shock. From what, I'm not sure since a lot has happened in the last five minutes.

"Yes," I answer, more sure than anything else before.

"Okay then, we'll make arrangements for banking and get

you a car here and a house. I'll start looking for housekeepers and—"

"Dad."

"Yes?"

"I don't want any of that. The house, the car, the housekeeper, or even the money."

"None of it?"

"None."

"But where will you live? I don't enjoy the idea of my daughter sleeping in the park again." His face wrinkles at the thought.

"You told him that?" I glance at Luke.

"Well … I … it was a heated moment and I wanted to make him feel like shit," he answers.

"It worked," my dad says.

"Good." Luke nods.

And that's the moment my father first smiles at Luke.

"As long as you're not sleeping on the street, let me know how I can help," my dad says, squeezing my wrist gently and turning for the door.

"One more thing." He pauses in the doorway to face me and Luke. "Your trust fund will always be yours to spend as you please, and I insist that you, at the very least, keep access to it for emergencies."

"Okay," I say, not arguing because the bookstore won't rebuild itself, and yes, taking the money feels wrong, but Luke deserves for someone to start looking out for him for a change. If being his sugar momma helps him out. I'll do it.

Luke gets out of his chair to kiss my cheek when my father is gone.

"Should we talk about what just happened?"

"No." I smile.

"You're okay?"

"I've never been better."

Still holding my hand, he sits back down.

As long as I'm with Luke, life will never be as amazing as it is now.

Turns out, the moment his sisters broke into the store and blamed it on me was the moment I needed in order to find Luke. It's a moment I'll never forget.

EPILOGUE

One month later ...

Skylar

Crutches and winter in Wyoming just don't mix.

Luke grabs my arms, again, to stabilize me on the ice.

"I told you I would just carry you in," he says.

"I know, but I need to learn how to do it on my own. You won't always be there for me when I need you. You still have a life, and we occasionally have different schedules."

"Yeah, I was actually wanting to talk to you about that," he says, slowing to a stop.

The BA's door flies open, and Beth pokes her head out.

"Hey there, roomie." She smiles at me.

Since the apartment above the bookstore isn't livable after the fire—at least not until the renovations on the building are done—I moved in with Beth. Luke wasn't very happy, but I didn't want to put any more problems on him. He repeatedly tells me I am not a problem. I still put my foot down. Even though Luke shows up every day, I lucked out that Beth was looking for a roommate.

"Think you could switch my clothes to the dryer when you go back home? I forgot earlier," she asks.

"Yeah, sure, but aren't you almost off?"

"I am, but I have a date."

"What? Who?" Luke and I ask in unison.

"None of your business." When she answers, she's staring at Luke and not me. I'm going to take that as a sign that she will tell me later.

"Well, you'll have to tell me all about it when you get home."

She responds with a wink.

"Okay, move, Beth. Sky needs to get out of the snow," Luke says, changing the subject.

"I won't break," I tell him as a crutch slips on the ice again.

"You just might." He laughs.

Beth holds the door open as we enter. It's the BA's post-Christmas Christmas party, so the place is closed except for friends or family members of those who work here.

Christmas decorations are everywhere. On the ceiling are those paper streamers I saw once in a movie. The ones made out of craft paper looped together. It doesn't take me long to spot the odd choice of colors.

"Shouldn't those be red and green or something?" I ask.

"Yeah, they probably should be, but I guess when Conner and Logan told the kids what to do, they left out mentioning using Christmas colors. Spring, fall, winter, and Christmas it is."

I laugh and it stings a little. Life has been a bit rough since I left the hospital. The good news is, I can see out of both eyes now that the swelling is down, and my lip is almost back to normal, enough at least that I can now kiss Luke anytime I want.

"Sky, over here," Beth calls out from where she stands in the corner with Sara and Kelsey. I don't know Kelsey very well, we only hung out with her a handful of times, but she is glowing. Luke said she and Ethan just found out they are expecting their third child in the spring. He also said not to drink the Parker or Brian water because those people are popping out kids like they're bubble gum.

I wanted to ask him if that means he doesn't want kids, but I figured it's too soon. Still, I'll probably keep away from the water.

"Hey, before you go over there, I thought I could give you your gift," Luke says. He disappears into the back room, returning quickly with a small yellow fuzz of a puppy in his arms.

"Oh my gosh." The tears start before I've got my balance, and Luke is handing me the dog. Once I have the puppy, Luke reaches into his pocket.

"There's more," he says.

My eyes widen and my heartbeat stumbles to stay steady when Luke settles his eyes on me.

He leans in to kiss me. It's short and sweet like all they've all been lately. He's scared he's going to be too rough with me, and it sucks. I miss the rough.

Turning my view to the small box in front of me, he slowly unties the bow. When the last piece of paper is gone, he pops open the small thin box. A key is sitting inside.

"I want to be the one to take care of you, Sky. Will you move in with me?"

"Yes!" I shout, my crutches falling to the ground as I wrap one arm around his neck and hold on to the puppy with the other.

I hear someone cheer, followed by a lot clapping. The noise is full of so much excitement, you'd would honestly think he was popping the question. I catch Beth's gaze in the corner of the room. Her bottom lip is bent down and her eyes are a mix of happy and sad.

I must have the same expression, because the next thing I know Luke takes the puppy—who I am looking forward to naming—and hands me my crutches as he nods in Beth's direction. I take a minute or two to hobble over to her.

"You know I can totally tell him I changed my mind."

She laughs. "That boy would die if you told him that, and you know it."

"True, but—" Something silver is sticking out of her purse, catching my attention. I reach for it and pull it out. Handcuffs—maybe I should have just asked instead of pulling them out.

Beth grabs them from my hand, blushing while she shoves them back in her purse, all while her gaze darts into every angle of the room. "Don't touch those," she says.

"Yeah, but who do you share them with?" I ask, trying not to laugh.

"I told you I have a date."

"How long have you been seeing this guy?"

It has to be a while if they are using handcuffs during sex. Then again, I slept with Luke on our first date, so I don't have much room to judge any one.

"Not long, but let's not talk about me. Let's talk about you and Luke."

"Or, we can all just enjoy the drinks and food and celebrate how lucky we are to be a part of lives of everyone who is here tonight," Ethan says. Luke is standing right being him.

He steps around Ethan and wraps me in a hug, kissing the top of my head. Ethan's right. I'm damn lucky to have all these people in my life. They've been the family I never had, and they just want me to be me and no one else. Glancing up at Luke, who is now looking down at me with a huge smile on his face, I know this is exactly where I was meant to be. With friends who love me for who I am, and with a man who would risk his life for me. These are the moments I want to remember. The moments when love conquers all.

Want more from Jami?
Subscribe to her mailing list for exclusive bonus epilogues and all the book news!

Are you ready for Beth's story, Just One Spark?
Keep reading for the first chapter!

JUST ONE SPARK
CHAPTER ONE

Beth

I haven't had sex in more than a year. Tonight, I have every intention of changing that. All the late nights of studying, constant emails between professors over assignments or potential careers, and leaving work or barbeques with friends early to make sure I'm getting everything with school finished have finally paid off. I've landed my dream job and it's time to celebrate—but more importantly, relax. And what better way than with some good old-fashioned one-night stand sex?

That should be easy to do, too, since I'm in Rockland, Colorado, visiting my good friend Liam—who, thankfully, is the only person here who knows me—and not back home in Wind Valley, Wyoming. Although, I'll be headed back tomorrow to prep for my first day as a working woman. It's a long stretch to get an assistant to the marketing director position straight out of college, but I'll be damned if I'm going to let all that hard work go to waste.

I scan the inside of the bar, searching for the perfect fling material. I come up short of prospects, taking in the fact it's only six in the evening and there aren't very many people here. There's a group of women in the corner near the bathroom hallway, wearing pastel pink, blue, and green dresses that just scream spring. Only two of the four pool tables lined against the back wall are being used, and there's a couple sitting at one of the round tables in the middle of the open room. Not a lot of choices for me at the moment.

"All I'm saying is that it's a risky move," Liam says. He's the manager, working behind the bar tonight at The Silver Tap. It's the sister bar to the one where I work in Wind Valley —now only weekends—The Black Alcove. That means free drinks for me. This is perfect, because as much as I am mentally shouting, "Yay, one-night stand," I'm also mentally shouting, "Don't do it. STD." Vodka and the splash of cranberry in front of me is definitely going to make one of those thoughts disappear. I mean, it's not like I'm going to go find the grimiest guy in the bar. I have standards, even if I say shit, fuck, and speak my mind way more than a person should. I don't really have a filter, but that has nothing to do with how I pick my men.

"I want to get laid, Liam. Since you and I have no attraction whatsoever, a stranger is going to have to do," I tell him. But I also prefer it this way. I want sex, not a relationship. Easy as that.

Liam squeezes his eyes closed and turns away from me. Probably thinking of how he attempted a night of lust but I just couldn't do it. Yeah, he's just under six feet, all muscle, and dark hair, dark eyes, but I don't know … maybe it's because I was friends with him first. That and my refusal to commit to a man—even when we go months without keeping in touch—could cost us our friendship. Anyway, every now and then, by the way he brushes an arm against me or voices his concerns about me always being alone or how I should see someone about my hesitation to jump into an actual relationship, I still think he has a thing for me. A small thing—I hope.

He releases a long sigh as he busies himself making drinks from the tickets he just tore off the printer. "At least pick the guy here, all right? Then I can see his face and maybe card him for his drink to memorize his address or something before you leave with a complete stranger who could murder you in the back of his car."

"First of all, I still have those handcuffs you gave me at Christmas." I pause, letting him laugh it off. It was a gag Christmas gift. Well, so he thinks. I really do plan to use them one day. "And second of all, you're being dramatic. That's not going to happen."

"You don't know that." He isn't laughing anymore.

"Considering I am planning on using the bathroom here or my room at your place, since that is where I'm staying, I do know."

"The bathroom, Beth, really?" he asks.

"At least you'll know where I am." I grin at him. I'm trying to help the guy release some of his discomfort with my evening plans. His lack of a smile says I'm not doing a good job.

A customer walks up a few stools down and Liam excuses himself to take care of the bald-headed man.

My phone lights up, as if my mother knows I have a free moment and was going to use it for something illicit. I let it ring.

It's not that I don't want to talk to her, but also that I don't.

If she wants to talk about something other than my dad, sure, I'd love to chat. But ever since my dad started dating someone new, she's been extra needy. Not to mention her drinking has increased. Right now, I want to tell her to suck it the fuck up. *You've been divorced for ten years. He's allowed to date again and so are you.* But of course, I'd never say any of that. My parents are the perfect example of why commitment is bullshit.

"So, tell me again how this new job works. They don't just hire you?" Liam asks once his customer has left.

"Yes, I'll going into the office every day and earn a paycheck, but I'm on a ninety-day trial. So yeah, if I don't earn the position, they let me go."

I really hope they don't.

"Do a lot of places do that?" he asks.

"I think it's more popular with bigger companies."

"What are you going to do if you don't make it?" he asks.

I sit up with my arms crossed in front of me. "What do you mean *if*, Liam? They'll keep me."

"But what if they don't?" he prompts.

"I need a new subject," I blurt out. "You're depressing me with your lack of excitement and clear confidence in me." Instead of the small sips I've been taking I start to gulp down the remainder of my drink. It would be fantastic if this liquor would work faster.

"Hey, I'm thrilled you got this marketing job. I know you've been working hard for it and I'm sure you'll keep it, but sex with a guy you don't know seems like a pretty manly way of celebrating."

"Whoa, sexist. What are you trying to say?" I unintentionally slam my glass against the counter.

He releases another sigh as the entrance door opens, streaming in the last little bit of daylight over his face as the sun is beginning to go down.

"Nothing. I take that back. It's just an odd way to handle victory is all," he says.

Victory.

I let the word settle in as a group of rowdy men step inside the bar. They're all donning suits and ties. But they look young. Possibly somewhere around my own age of twenty-five. Thirty, max. One man stands out in the crowd, not only because he's the only one to wander to the music box, but because he is the only one who has well-groomed scruff that covers his face. It's shaved so perfectly that his jawline is more pronounced than normal. I've never been a fan of facial hair, but tonight, I think I could be.

He taps away at the screen, searching for what I hope is a song I'll enjoy. After all, he did just cut off the playlist I lined up on the damn thing. Took me over an hour, too.

Bands. Every bar should stick to live bands.

He shifts from his right foot to his left, sliding every finger but his thumb into his right pocket. His left thumb of his other hand rests against his lips as he pauses. I like those lips. They aren't too plump and they aren't so thin that I'll feel like I'm kissing his chin more so than his mouth. They look like nice kissing lips. His tongue glides over them, leaving a glistening coat. Yes, those are positively kissable lips. I'm still staring when he turns. He must have sensed he was being watched because a pair of bold, golden brown eyes settle right on me. He smiles and then winks. I twist back around to face Liam.

"Looks like you found your guy," he says, full on rolling his eyes at me like a girl.

"No, I'll keep looking," I say.

"Why? He is clearly into you?"

"Yeah, he also caught me looking at him, which means he thinks I'm into him, which also makes him think I'll be easy."

"But you're specifically searching for a man to have sex with. What am I missing here?" Liam asks.

"Yeah, well I still want the guy to work for it. I mean this" —I point to my face and my body—"is not just something you get. You have to earn it." I'm not conceited, but I know every woman, beautiful or flawed, deserves to be wooed properly. No matter the circumstance. And tonight, even though I'm not going to focus on any part of my life but sex, I still want to feel wanted by whoever I choose. The trick now is finding the right guy and turning tonight into one of the best nights of my life.

Maverick

"You slept with our client's wife."

My father, who doubles as my boss, paces behind his desk. He's not asking a question. He already knows the answer. It's more like he's waiting for me to confirm the accusation. Which I will, because it's true. I just hate that I've disappointed him. Again. It's like senior year when I told him I wanted to follow in his footsteps in the family marketing business instead of taking the college football scholarship in Tennessee. Most fathers would have been thrilled. Not mine.

He had to have known I would make that choice. He

interned me with the company every summer since eighth grade, and some nights after school, we'd sit and spitball ideas back and forth for hours. I never did it as an excuse to spend time with him after mom died in my junior year of high school; I did it because he loved it, and because he loved it, so did I. So now I'm here, eight years later, working with him and struggling to accept that what I did shouts how much I haven't grown up.

"I didn't know she was his wife. Most wives attend the meetings instead of waiting in reception," I say.

His stride stops and he turns to face me, leaning forward, palms flat against his desk. "You cost the company a seven-figure deal, Maverick."

He had to remind me. I've beaten myself up more than anyone over this since six days ago when this same mentioned woman came into our office, bringing her husband to meet me so he'd know she wasn't lying. I'd say they had some problems going on at home and I was her ticket out. But no matter their issues, I'm the one who made the mistake.

"Had I known who she was, it wouldn't have happened." I lean back in my seat, cross one ankle over the opposite knee, and loosen the collar of my shirt. "You know I would never intentionally cost us a contract."

Closing a seven-figure deal will always get my blood pumping. No matter how many times I've watched the owner of a company sign his name after I've pitched him the most brilliant marketing proposal he'll ever hear, it never gets old. I'm not a cocky jackass like most people think; I'm just good at my job. Extremely good. Others—coworkers, friends, people I meet in passing—choose to call me a jerk rather than admit they wish they could do their job the way I do. I have a

95 percent success rate. Who doesn't want to say that about themselves?

Most people think I'm in this position because my own father is the president of this company, Mitchell Marketing. The degrees hanging on the wall behind my desk in my office say otherwise.

"No, no I don't know that. Not with these juvenile actions," he says.

His hard stare matches my own.

"Dad, I've closed more contracts than almost everyone here combined. Not including you, of course."

Great, now I'm mixing a little bit of whining with bragging. This is not my style.

"Sealing the deal doesn't mean anything if you don't have respect for our company. Your uncle and I didn't create this business for our kids to come in here and tarnish the hardworking and loyal reputation we've built."

"That's all Austin's doing," I say. My cousin is a spoiled idiot who blows through my uncle's money doing everything he can to avoid growing up.

"After this stunt, I'm not so sure he's alone."

"Dad—"

"Maverick, I've always known you love marketing. I knew you'd be great at making the pitch to our clients and that you'd be the best man to replace me as president when I retire, which is why I hired you as soon as you had your degree. But now, I'm not so sure I made the right choice."

"Whoa, Dad, I messed up. I know I did, but you don't need to fire me." I sit up, resting my arms on my thighs. "I'll find a way to make back the number we lost. You can trust me."

A sly smile crosses my father's lips, the same one he used to display after my games in high school when he'd hear people talking about what a great arm I had. He's always loved knowing something other people didn't.

"I know I can, and that is exactly why first thing Monday morning, you will start new hire recruitment for the assistant to marketing director position in Wind Valley under your uncle's guidance."

I sleep with a client's wife and instead of punishing me, he sends me to Wyoming to choose who the next person we hire is?

"Uncle Bart wants me there?" I ask. I haven't seen the man since my graduation. Talked to him on the phone and emailed him through the company for business, yes, but on a personal level, no. And not once in any of our work conversations did he show any type of acceptance of me. Mostly because I was able to skip the recruitment phase myself. I got lucky. Although, I have no doubt I would have come out as the best recruit for whatever job they were hiring for at the time.

"Of course he does. In fact, he was the one who mentioned the idea to me," Dad answers.

"Wow, I don't know what to say. I'm honored you have that much faith in me. I won't let you down. I'll pick the best candidate." I stand, straighten my tie, and turn for the door.

"Maverick."

"Yeah?" I twist back around.

"You're not going to be selecting a recruit."

"I'm not?"

"No, you are one of the recruits."

I blank on any response.

"Prove to me and this company in the next ninety days that you want to be here and I'll bring you back to Colorado. You can resume your current position as VP project director, and we can discuss the idea of my retirement in the next couple of years. If you don't succeed in earning your place back, then you no longer have a job here."

"I made one mistake; it's not going to happen again," I repeat myself.

"Then you should have no problem proving that to everyone else in the company who will one day, hopefully, look up to you as an employer." He nods, once, his clear tell sign that this discussion is over. I return his nod and again head for the door.

"One last thing," his voice stops me. "You've got to start placing the needs of the company before your own in certain areas. Your love life and career need to be fully separate. Mixing the two is the perfect recipe for disaster."

"Yes, sir," I say with no hesitation and finally leave his office.

Don't worry, Dad. If mixing sex and business together is going to set me back every time, I can guarantee it will not happen again.

I follow a group of men inside the bar. The men, like me, are all sporting suits. I've heard that downtown Rockland includes more office buildings in a five-block radius than most other cities in the northeastern part of the state. The Silver Tap, the bar I'm walking into right now, is conveniently in the middle of those five blocks. Whoever opened this business right here knew the opportunities a placement like this would provide them. The average working human enjoys a drink after work. This location is a brilliant move if you ask me, considering I fall into average right now.

The crowd that enters in front of me veers to the left, claiming the table nearest the door. I take a quick scan of the room. I'm meeting my sister, Tiffany, for drinks, possibly two. She wants to talk about what happened. Not as head of human resources but as my sister.

I spot a jukebox out of the corner of my eye and head that direction. I press a few buttons and ponder my choices of music: country, rock, rap, and more. It's a basic selection. I settle on some oldies. A rack of pool balls breaking rattles behind me. A round sounds like a great distraction, considering my sister is going to jump right into the discussion of what she thinks I should do when I get to the office on Monday.

I look over my shoulder to see if there is an empty pool table, but I don't get a chance to find a free table before a solemn woman with fiery red hair who's seated at the bar grabs my attention. She's staring right at me and doesn't even flinch once I send her a wink and grin. All things considered, finding a random hookup isn't the best choice to make right now, but hell, I may as well go all out tonight if I'm going to be all business for the rest of the summer.

Red's expression doesn't change before she twists back around. The bartender braces his arms against the bar top before saying something to her.

She flips her hair over her shoulder where it ends gracefully at the middle of her lower back. She wearing black shoes that could easily be mistaken for socks. Her dark blue jeans are ripped at the knees and her black t-shirt barely meets the waistband of her pants. She looks over her shoulder once more and I barely catch the spark of emerald in her eyes before she reverts her gaze forward again.

My type has always been suits and success, but something about this woman won't let me pull my eyes away.

"Can I get you something?" a blonde waitress in a navy mini skirt asks.

"No, I'm all right. Thanks. I'm just going to have a seat at the bar," I answer. She nods and passes me to her next table.

There are about ten empty barstools at the bar, but I head straight for the one beside Red.

The bartender shifts away from her to greet me. "What can I get ya?" he asks.

"I'll take a Coors Original, please," I say and steal a glance at the woman next to me.

She makes a gagging gesture with her finger before she turns to me. "Of all the beers you could pick, you pick the most repulsive one available."

I chuckle. "And what would you have recommended?" The bartender hands me my beer and I take a swig, waiting for Red's answer.

"Maybe a Sam Adams or something else not so boring."

"Boring," I repeat. "I've actually never been told that my taste of any kind is … boring."

Her lips twitch right before she licks them and narrows her eyes at me. I hadn't been expecting her to be so quickly responsive to my comment.

"I take it we've moved past talking about beer," she says.

"Well, did you want to continue small talk or get right to point of why I sat next to you?"

Her gaze flashes between me and the bartender, who is now at the other end of the bar and not paying attention to us.

"I'm going to step outside for some air. Would you like to join me?" she asks, spinning on her chair and standing.

I chug the remainder of my beer and rise. "I'd love to."

Ninety-five percent perfect success rate.

I follow behind her, catching the moment she glances back to the bartender, again. I do the same and am struck with arms folded across his chest and a glare. Perhaps I should be worried that I'm about to steal another man's woman for a bit, but if they were actually together, he would have been over the bar top by now with his fist in my face. I mean, if I had a girl who looked like the one with the swaying hips in front of me, I'd work overtime to make sure men knew she was mine.

We step outside and Red heads straight for the side of the building. The second I turn the corner she pushes me up against the faded red brick. I expect her to dive right into kissing me, but she doesn't. The way her sultry eyes roam over my body makes the decision of what to do next for me.

My lips capture hers and my tongue invades her mouth before she can protest. Bracing my hands on her hips, I spin us around. I lift her and she wraps her legs around me before it's her turn to be pressed against the wall.

Her hands rest on my face as she kisses me harder. Her fingers curl in my hair, and the way the tips massage my scalp each time her tongue collides with mine sends a newfound sense of desire from my head all the way to my toes. The evidence of how much I'm enjoying this presses against her stomach, only fueling her kisses. We're basically rubbing against each other where anyone can see us. A splice of jealousy that someone could see her like this when it should be meant only for me runs through my body. No woman has ever given me a single thought even close to that one, and I pull away.

Warm eyes gaze up at me. I lean down to kiss her once more and then release her legs till her feet are planted back on the ground.

Red bites her bottom lip and the action makes me dip to take over for her. I could kiss her all day long.

"Your place or mine?" she says before I get the chance.

A woman who knows what she wants. Man, this one just keeps getting sexier and sexier.

"If we exchange names, that might—"

"Make things complicated," she finishes for me. "Look, if you don't want to do this, I don't care."

"No, I do," I say a bit too eagerly. I take her hand and start to lace our fingers so I can lead her back to my place—probably the worst idea I've ever had—a couple blocks away when she jerks her hand away from my touch.

"Sex. Just sex. No hand holding or anything else."

"It was an innocent move," I say, holding back a laugh.

Instead of taking off for my place, I press my body into her, my legs parting hers as I lean forward, kissing just under her ear.

"I don't want commitment. If you're looking for one night with a guy who will treat you right and put all your needs before his, I'm your man. I've never been arrested and I have a clean bill of health. I'm twenty-six and my name is—"

"Stop." She holds up a hand and smiles. "The less we know about each other, the better."

A smile tugs at my lips. "Really, no names?"

"No names," she repeats.

She full out wants to have a complete one-night stand. I'm not sure whether I should be appalled or impressed.

A growl comes from deep in my throat as my lips devour hers again. Her head falls back the best it can as I kiss down her neck to her chest. I lift one leg to my side, allowing myself to grind into her, a preview for later.

Later must not be something she wants, because her hands glide under my jacket and before I know it, she has unlatched my belt and pulled down my zipper.

"You can't be serious!" Both Red's body and my own freeze at the high-pitched shrill behind us. "I'm ten minutes late and you've already moved on to new plans for the night."

I immediately twist my body to shield Red and the display of my very pronounced erection.

"What are you doing? Oh, my god!" My sister yells one more time as she observes me and Red with a furious gaze.

"Tiff, stop yelling" is how I start but am immediately cut off from saying any more.

"You have a girlfriend!" Red scolds and shoves me back.

"What?" I ask and jerk my pants back into place. "No … I—"

"You're a pig," Red snaps, yanking her shirt back down.

"Wait," I call out just as she is almost around the corner. "I don't have a girlfriend. That wasn't—"

"Yeah, clearly you don't now that she caught you."

"No, I mean, can we just try this again?"

My sister lets out a huff as she crosses her arms, glaring at Red while she watches our interaction. That certainly doesn't help.

"You're kidding, right? One-night stands are supposed to be easy. This was a train wreck, and thank fucking god I never have to see you or your girlfriend again. All girls deserve more than what your sleezeball ass has to offer."

With that, she marches back inside the bar.

I slouch back against the wall. Well, that was a disaster, but I can't say it was the first time that's ever happened to me. It is, however, the first time I want to tell my sister to fuck off.

"Mav, you can't be distracting yourself with a woman right now. Might I remind you that's how you got yourself into this mess?"

I press the heel of my palm into my eyes. "It was just sex, Tiff."

"I'm sure it was," she says, placing her hands on her hips as she glares at me. "You want the president spot, you need to be focused."

"If I want sex in my life, Tiff, no one is going to tell me I can't." I push off the wall and look down the street. I'll need another bar if I want some drinks.

"Mav," she says, her tone laced and ready for an argument.

"Tiff." There isn't anything she can say about this entire situation at work that I haven't already told myself.

We have one of our typical brother sister stare downs that usually end with her winning. Not this time.

"Fine," she snaps. "You're right."

"I know I'm right," I say. She shoves me as we walk away from The Silver Tap.

"You might be a little right, too," I say. "I've let Dad down enough this last week. I don't plan on doing it again."

"Ever the family man, that guy," she replies. "He just wants what's best for you, Mav."

It's true, Dad is all about running a successful business,

but he's even more about having a family. He wants it for both of his kids, but neither of us have made that commitment yet. And I sure as shit haven't been going about it the right way.

I take a look over my shoulder as we make our way down the street. I could go back, explain Tiff is my sister, and probably get back to where I left off with Red, but that's a lot of work for one night of sex. And besides, I need to focus on developing an approach to the next three months. I'm not letting this job slip out of my hands. That's what I should be worrying about, not thinking about how the most gorgeous woman I've ever met now thinks I'm the world's largest scumbag. I should probably just pretend this evening never happened and feel lucky that the chances of ever seeing her again are slim to none.

Keep reading Just One Spark today!

Don't want to miss out on any new releases from Jami?
Subscribe to her mailing list for exclusive bonus epilogues
and all the book news!

MORE BOOKS BY JAMI ROGERS

The Black Alcove Series

Just One Kiss

Just One Night

Just One Touch

Just One Moment

Just One Spark

Just One Love

The Kiss Me Crazy Series

Kiss Me Crazy

Love is Crazy

I Want Crazy

The Evergreen Brothers Series

A Boyfriend by Christmas

The Summer Wedding Hoax

A Match by Christmas

The Lust or Bust Series

The Write One

Write About You

The Write Choice

Write That Down

More Than Write

Always Been Write

Standalone Novels

Love Money

Date in the Dark (A New Years Eve Novella)

ACKNOWLEDGMENTS

Like the last book in this series, this one also took me three plotlines to find the perfect one for Skylar and Luke. Each one holds a place in my heart, but their final story is one I will never forget. Writing it challenged me in many ways, and since I typed that last word, I have been eager to share this book. I know the names mentioned below are mentioned in almost every book I write, but they are my writing family, my team. None of this would be possible without them.

Dana Volney – You are always mentioned first, and that is because you endure the most of my thoughts, my struggles, and my excitement when I things start to come together. You read my books after I've written the most beautifully painful copy ever, and yet you still respond as if I just wrote a novel that changed your life. Your pumped spirit when we talk about my books is all I need to remember why I do this—because I love it. Thank you.

Grant Rogers: Oh, my future husband. Thank you for being patient, for being supportive, and mostly for accepting that you're marrying a woman who has a mind filled with hundreds of personalities just waiting to come out. Our lives will never lack excitement, and I can't wait to be Mrs. Rogers. I love you!

Mom and Dad: You move in less than a month, and I am

going to miss you more than I'll ever show it. I love you. Thank you for raising me to never give up.

Holly: Even if we don't talk every day, I miss you every day. I love you, and I can't wait to see you soon.

Julie Sturgeon: I think your section is the hardest to write, you know, because you get to edit it. The way you help my books go from good to fabulous never gets old. Your work is phenomenal, and I am so very lucky that Dana recommended you to me. Everything you do gives me the confidence I need when a book is released. Together, I know we always do our best. Thank you.

Potter Sorenson Photography: Your work is fabulous, and I couldn't have found anyone better if I tried. Can wait to work with you in the future!

Alyssa, Christian, and Trisha: You never judge, you never doubt, and you are always there when I need you. You understand me more than I ever thought you could. Seriously, you are the best friends a girl could ever ask for. Christian, if you are reading this, have I ever told you how much you would enjoy living in Wyoming?

Megan: Thank you for being a crazy awesome friend. We've been friends for almost five years now. April 13 is our friendiversary, in case you didn't know. I know this because I started work on Friday the 13th. Pretty sure we didn't become insta-friends on this day though, due to your "don't talk to me before nine a.m." rule. However, it was super close to that date because, lucky you, I never did well following that rule. Eight a.m. would come around, and HELLO MEGAN! But most importantly, thank you for being there for me on such short notice because you see me stressing and want to help.

People like you make my life so much easier. I'll always find ways to make it up to you.

And finally, thank you to the readers, bloggers, and social media fans who are reading the Black Alcove series and spreading the word. Everything you do to support me and my dream is amazing!

ABOUT THE AUTHOR

My name is Jami Rogers and I write new adult contemporary and adult contemporary romance novels. I *love* love and want to share my passion for happily ever afters with the world.

I was born in Wyoming and still live in the cowboy state with my husband, daughter, and two dogs. I like to read, write, run, watch movies/TV and spend time with my family. I'm horrible at returning phone calls and prefer to text, but still struggle to hit the little blue arrow to send a message once I'm finished typing my reply. My husband does 90% of the cooking in our house. Not because I'm busy – I'm just simply a bad cook.

Keep up with Jami by visiting her website www.authorjamirogers.com
or
Subscribe to her mailing list for exclusive bonus epilogues and all the book news!